Aerogrammes

and other stories

Aerogrammes
and other stories

TANIA JAMES

ALFRED A. KNOPF · NEW YORK · 2012

THIS IS A BORZOI BOOK
PUBLISHED BY ALFRED A. KNOPF

All rights reserved. Published in the United States by Alfred A. Knopf,
a division of Random House, Inc., New York, and in Canada
by Random House of Canada Limited, Toronto.
www.aaknopf.com

Knopf, Borzoi Books, and the colophon are
registered trademarks of Random House, Inc.

Portions of this work were originally published in the following: "The Gulf"
in *Boston Review;* "Girl Marries Ghost," in very different form, in *The
Courier-Journal;* "Escape Key" in *Five Chapters;* "Ethnic Ken" and "Light &
Luminous" in *Five Points;* "Lion and Panther in London" in *Granta;* "What to
Do with Henry" in *Kenyon Review;* "Aerogrammes" in *One Story;* and "*The
Scriptological Review:* A Last Letter from the Editor" in *A Public Space.*

Library of Congress Cataloging-in-Publication Data
James, Tania.
Aerogrammes : and other stories / Tania James.
p.   cm.
ISBN 978-0-307-26891-4 (hardback)
I. Title.
PS3610.A458A68 2012   813'.6—dc23   2011033755

Front-of-jacket illustration by Steven Attardo
Jacket design by Barbara de Wilde

Manufactured in the United States of America
First Edition

For Vivek

Contents

· · ·

Aerogrammes

and other stories

Lion and Panther in London

. . .

The Sensation of the Wrestling World
Exclusive Engagement of India's
Catch-as-Catch-Can Champions.
Genuine Challengers of the Universe.
All Corners. Any Nationality. No One Barred.

GAMA, Champion undefeated wrestler of India, winner of
over 200 legitimate matches.

IMAM, his brother, Champion of Lahore.

(These wrestlers are both British subjects.)

£5 will be presented to any competitor, no matter what
nationality, whom any member of the team fails to throw in
five minutes.

Gama, the Lion of the Punjab, will attempt to throw any
three men, without restriction as to weight, in 30 minutes,

any night during this engagement, and competitors are
asked to present themselves, either publicly or
through the management.

NO ONE BARRED!! ALL CHAMPIONS CORDIALLY INVITED!!
THE BIGGER THE BETTER!!

Gama the Great is bored. Imam translates the newspaper notice as best he can while his brother slumps in the wing-back chair. On the table between them rests a rose marble chessboard, frozen in play. Raindrops wriggle down the windowpane. It is a mild June in 1910 and their seventh day in London without a single challenge.

Their tour manager, Mr. Benjamin, lured them here from Lahore, promising furious bouts under calcium lights, their names in every newspaper that matters. But the very champions who used to thump their chests and flex their backs for photos are now staying indoors, as if they have ironing to do. Not a word from Benjamin "Doc" Roller or Strangler Lewis, not from the Swede Jon Lemm or the whole fleet of Japanese fresh from Tokyo.

Every year in London, a world champion is crowned anew, one white man after the next, none of whom have wrestled a *pehlwan.* They know nothing of Handsome Hasan or Kalloo or the giant Kikkar Singh, who once uprooted an acacia tree bare-handed, just because it was disrupting the view from his window. Gama has defeated them all, and more, but how is he to be Champion of the World if this half of the world is in hiding?

Mr. Benjamin went to great trouble to arrange the trip. He cozied up to the Mishra family and got the Bengali millionaires to finance the cause, printed up press releases, and rented them a small, gray-shingled house removed from the thick of the city, with space enough out back to carry on their training. The house is fairly comfortable, if crowded with tables, standing lamps, settees, and armchairs. When it rains, they push the furniture to the walls and conduct their routines in the center of the sitting room.

Other adjustments are not so easy. Gama keeps tumbling out of bed four hours late, his mustache squashed on one side. Imam climbs upon the toilet bowl each morning, his feet on the rim, and engages in a bout with his bowels. Afterward, he inspects the results. If they are coiled like a snake ready to strike, his guru used to say, all is in good shape. There are no snakes in London.

These days, when Mr. Benjamin stops by, he has little more to offer than an elaborate salaam and any issues of *Sporting Life* and *Health & Strength* in which they have been mentioned, however briefly. He is baby-faced and bald, normally jovial, but Imam senses something remote about him, withheld, as though the face he gives them is only one of many. "You and your theories," Gama says.

Left to themselves, Gama and Imam continue to hibernate in the melancholy house. They run three kilometers up and down the road, occasionally coughing in the fume and grumble of a motorcar. They wrestle. They do hundreds of *bethaks* and *dands,* lost in the calm that comes of repetition, and at the end of the day, they rest. They bathe. They smooth their skin with dry mustard, which conjures homeward thoughts of plains ablaze with yellow blooms. Sometimes, reluctantly, they play another game of chess.

On the eighth morning, Mr. Benjamin pays a visit. For the first time in their acquaintance, he looks agitated and fidgets with his hat. His handshake is damp. He follows the wrestlers into the sitting room, carrying with him the stink of a recently smoked cigar.

The cook brings milky yogurt and ghee for the wrestlers, tea for Mr. Benjamin. Gama and Imam brought their own cook from Lahore, old Ahmed, who is deaf in one ear but knows every nuance of the *pehlwan* diet. They were warned about English food: mushy potatoes, dense pies, gloomy puddings—the sort of fare that would render them leaden in body and mind.

When Mr. Benjamin has run out of small talk, he empties a sober sigh into his cup. "Right. Well, I suppose you're wondering about the tour."

"Yes, quite," Imam says, unsure of his words but too anxious to care. It seems a bad sign when Mr. Benjamin sets his cup and saucer aside.

Wrestling in England, Mr. Benjamin explains, has become something of a business. Wrestlers are paid to take a fall once in a while, to pounce and pound and growl on cue, unbeknownst to the audience, which nevertheless seems to enjoy the drama. After the match, the wrestlers and their managers split the money. Occasionally these hoaxes are discovered, to great public outcry, the most recent being the face-off between Yousuf the Terrible Turk and Stanislaus Zbyszko. After Zbyszko's calculated win, it was revealed that Yousuf the Terrible was actually a Bulgarian named Ivan with debts to pay off.

"And you know of this now only?" Imam asks.

"No—well, not entirely." Mr. Benjamin pulls on a finger, absently cracks his knuckle. "I thought I could bring you fellows and turn things around. Show everyone what the sport bloody well should be."

Imam glances at Gama, who is leaning forward, gazing at Mr. Benjamin's miserable face with empathy.

"There would be challengers"—Mr. Benjamin shrugs—"if only you would agree to take a fall here and there."

After receiving these words from Imam, Gama pulls back, as if bitten. "Fall how?" Gama says.

"On purpose," Imam explains quietly.

Gama's mouth becomes small and solemn. Imam tells Mr. Benjamin that they will have to decline the offer.

"But you came all this way." Mr. Benjamin gives a flaccid laugh. "Why go back with empty pockets?"

For emphasis, Mr. Benjamin pulls his own lint-ridden pockets inside out and nods at Gama with the sort of encouragement one might show a thick-headed child.

Gama asks Imam why Mr. Benjamin is exposing the lining of his pants.

"The *langot* we wear, it does not have pockets," Imam tells Mr. Benjamin, hoping the man might appreciate the poetry of his refusal. Mr. Benjamin blinks at him and explains, in even slower English, what he means by "empty pockets."

So this is London, Imam thinks, nodding at Mr. Benjamin. A city where athletes are actors, where the ring is a stage.

In a final effort, Mr. Benjamin takes their story to the British press. *Health & Strength* publishes a piece entitled "Gama's Hopeless Quest for an Opponent," while *Sporting Life* runs his full-length photograph alongside large-lettered text: "GAMA, the great Indian Catch-Can Wrestler, whose Challenges to Meet all the Champions have been Unanswered." The photographer encouraged Gama to strike a menacing pose, but in the photo, Gama appears flat-footed and blank, his fists feebly raised, a stance that wouldn't menace a pigeon.

Finally, for an undisclosed sum, Doc Roller takes up Gama's challenge. Mr. Benjamin says that Doc is a fully trained doctor and the busiest wrestler in England, a fortunate combination for him because he complains of cracked ribs after every defeat.

They meet at the Alhambra, a sprawling pavilion of arches and domes, its name studded in bulbs that blaze halos through the fog. Inside, golden foliage and gilded trees climb the walls. Men sit shoulder to shoulder around the roped-off ring, and behind them, more men in straw boaters and caps, standing on bleachers, making their assessments of Gama the Great, the dusky bulk of his chest, the sculpted sandstone of each thigh. Imam sits ringside next to Mr. Benjamin, in a marigold robe and turban. He is a vivid blotch in a sea of grumpy grays and browns. He feels slightly overdressed.

Gama warms his muscles by doing *bethaks*. He glances up but keeps squatting when Roller swings his long legs over the ropes, dauntingly tall, and whips off his white satin robe to reveal wrestling pants, his abdominal muscles like bricks stacked above the waistband.

They take turns on the scale. Doc is a full head taller and exceeds Gama by thirty-four pounds. Following the announcement of their weights, the emcee bellows, "No money in the world would ever buy the Great Gama for a fixed match!" To this, a hailstorm of whooping applause.

Imam absently pinches the silk of his brother's robe, which is draped across his lap. Every time he watches his brother in a match, a familiar disquiet spreads through his stomach, much like the first time he witnessed Gama in competition.

Imam was eight, Gama twelve, when their uncle brought them to Jodhpur for the national strong-man competition. Raja Jaswant Singh had gathered hundreds of men from all across India to see who could last the longest drilling *bethaks*. The competitors took their places on the square field of earth within the palace courtyard, and twelve turbaned royal guards stood sentinel around the grounds, their tall gold spears glinting in the sun. Spectators formed a border some meters away from the field, and when little Gama emerged from their ranks and joined the strong men, laughter trailed behind him. Gama was short for his age but hale and sturdy even then.

When the raja raised his hand, Gama began, up and down, steady as a piston. His gaze never wavered, fixed on a single point of concentration in the air before him, as if his competitors and critics had all dissolved into the heat. At some point, Imam wanted to sit in the shade, but his uncle refused to move, too busy staring at Gama, as if with every *bethak*, the boy was transforming into something winged and brilliant. When Imam complained about the sun, his uncle said, "Look at your *bhaiya*. Does he complain?"

Imam looked at his brother: serene and focused, impervious to pain—everything Imam was not. There was a gravity about Gama in his youth, as if he had been schooled from the womb in the ways of the *pehlwan*, to avoid extremes of emotion like rage and lust, to reserve his energies for the pit. Their father had begun Gama's training at age five and died three years later, before Imam could prove himself worthy of the same attention.

The *bethak* contest lasted four hours, and by the end, only fifteen men remained standing. Raja Singh yanked Gama's hand into the air, declaring him the youngest by far and, thus, the winner. Greased in sweat, Gama wore a funny, dreamy expression, listing slightly before his knees buckled. Seeing him this way—limp, waxy, the crescent whites of his eyes between his lashes—made something jerk in Imam's chest. He could not move. At that moment, Imam began to hate his uncle. He hated the raja for coming up with this contest, and he hated every person who herded around his brother and blocked out the sun, claiming him as if he were theirs.

·

The bell clangs, and the match with Roller begins. Gama slaps his thighs, beats his chest, charges. He plunges at Doc's leg. Doc evades him the first time, but not the second. With a smooth back heel, Gama fells him and finishes him off with a half nelson and a body roll. One minute and forty seconds.

The second fall happens in but a blur—Doc laid out on his belly, sweat-slick and wincing at the spectators in the front row, who lean forward with their elbows on their knees. Roller gives in, and then: bedlam. The emcee yanks Gama's hand into the air; men mob the mat like sparrows to a piece of bread. Mr. Benjamin wrings Imam's hand, then shoulders his way through the crowd. Imam hangs back, Gama's robe in his arms, craning his neck to see over all the hats and heads between him and his brother.

Over the next few days, Gama defeats two more challengers, sends them staggering to the mat like drunken giants. The newspapers have begun to take notice. Sometimes, while warming up, Gama and Imam spot a reporter watching from the road, the brim of his hat shadowing his eyes as he scribbles something in his notebook. Imam doesn't like being ogled while doing his *dands,* but Mr. Benjamin has told them not to shoo the scribblers away. Press, he says, breeds more press.

Mr. Benjamin is right. These days, he brings more clippings than ever before, and Gama wants to digest every word, his appetite inexhaustible. Imam would rather play chess, the only game at which he consistently beats his brother. The journalists rarely, if ever, mention him.

"Gama the Great," writes Percy Woodmore in *Health & Strength,* "has so handily defeated all his European challengers that one can only wonder whether the Oriental strong man possesses some genetic advantage over his Occidental counterpart." Imam can recognize barely half the words in this sentence, but he understands the next: "Will the Hindoos ever lose?"

"Do you know," Gama interjects, "these sahibs have so few counters—only *one* to the cross-buttock hold." Gama shakes his head in bemusement, and just when Imam thinks he cannot stand him a minute longer, Gama adds, "Wait till they see you in the ring."

Imam is beginning to wonder if that day will ever arrive. He feels the distinct weight of malaise, same as he used to suffer in school. When they were children, Gama got to train at the *akhara* with Madho Singh, while Imam had to recite English poems about English flowers. After Gama's triumph at Jodhpur, people talked as if the boy could upend mountains, greater than all the *pehlwan* ancestors who had preceded him.

Sometimes, if Imam was sitting alone, sullenly reciting his multiplication tables, Gama took pity on him. "Come on, *chotu*," he'd say, taking Imam outside to show him a new hold. Gama was the only one who called him *chotu*, a word that raised his spirits when nothing else would.

By age twelve, Imam was fed up. He began cutting school and hovering around the *akhara*, where the only language that mattered was the heave and grunt of bodies in constant motion, whether climbing the rope hanging from the neem tree, or hoeing the wrestling pit, or swinging a giant *jori* in each arm, spiky clubs that surpassed him in height. Moving, always moving. The *akhara* seemed a splendid hive unto itself, sealed off from mundane concerns like school and exams and the sting of the teacher's switch. Here was his classroom. Here, among the living, was where he belonged.

•

Finally Mr. Benjamin arranges a match for Imam. He is to take on the Swede Jon Lemm, who has won belts from both the Alhambra and Hengler's tournaments.

They meet at the Alhambra once again, to a sold-out arena. Imam has the advantage of height but feels gangly next to Lemm, who is a stout tangle of muscle, and pale, with eyes of a clear, celestial blue.

The referee summons them to the center of the mat. Lemm gives a cordial nod and locks Imam in a hard handshake before releasing him to his corner. Imam can feel the spectators watching him, murmuring. One fellow openly points at Gama, who seems not to notice, sitting beside Mr. Benjamin with an air of equanimity. There is a proverb that their forefathers minded for centuries: *Make your mind as still as the bottom of a well, your body as hard as its walls.*

Imam touches the mat, then his heart.

The bell clangs, and Lemm hurls himself at Imam; his back heel topples Imam onto his back. Imam slips free, darts around Lemm, quick as the crack of a whip. He does not see Lemm in terms of ankle and knee and leg. Instead he tracks Lemm's movements, listening for one false note—the falter, the doubt, the dread.

At one point Lemm stalls, a fatal mistake. Imam lunges, lifts him up, and hurls him to the mat. He flips the bucking Swede and pins him. Three minutes and one second.

Not long into the second bout, Lemm is sprawled out on the mat, Imam on his back. Imam can feel Lemm struggling beneath him, trembling down to his deepest tissues until, with a savage groan, he deflates. One minute and eight seconds.

Imam gets to his feet, heaving. Something bounces lightly

off his back. He whirls around to find a beheaded flower at his feet. Someone else tosses him a silver pocket watch. Imam turns from one side to the other; the men are roaring. It takes him a dizzying moment to realize they are roaring for him.

Of the fight with Lemm, a reporter from *Health & Strength* goes into rapture: "That really was a wonderful combat— a combat in which both men wrestled like masters of the art. . . . Let us have a few more big matches like unto that, and I tell you straight that the grappling game will soon become the greatest game of all."

In the two weeks that follow, Gama and Imam defeat every wrestler who will accept the challenge. Though Gama the Great commands the most public attention, a dedicated sect of Imam devotees takes shape. They mint him with a new name: the Panther of the Punjab. They contend that the Panther is really the superior of the two, citing the blur of his bare brown feet, so nimble they make an elephant of every opponent. Gama may be stronger, but Imam has the broader arsenal of holds and locks and throws, as seen in his victories over Deriaz and Cherpillod, the latter Frenchman so frustrated that he stomped off to his dressing room midway through the match and refused to come out. Within a year or two, they claim, Imam will surpass Gama.

Gama listens in silence when Imam relays such passages. He betrays no emotion, though his fingers tend to tap against his glass of yogurt milk.

Baron Helmuth von Baumgarten is the only critic to speak in political terms, a realm unfamiliar to both Gama and Imam. "If the Indian wrestlers continue to win," the baron writes, with typical inflammatory flair, "their victories will spur on those dusky subjects who continue to menace the integrity of the British Empire."

And where most articles include a photo of Gama or Imam, this one displays a photo of a young Indian man in an English suit, with sculpted curls around a center part as straight as a blade. This is Madan Lal Dhingra, the baron explains, a student who, several months earlier, walked into an open street, revolver in hand, and shot a British government official seven times in the face. Before Dhingra could turn the revolver on himself, he was subdued, arrested, tried, and hanged.

Imam looks over Gama's shoulder at the article. They stare in silence at the soft-skinned boy with the starched white collar choking his throat. He looks much like the interpreters who sometimes tag along with the English journalists, a few stitches of hair across their upper lips, still boys to the mothers they must have left behind.

Gama folds the paper roughly, muttering, "Half of it is nonsense, what they write." He tosses the newspaper on the coffee table and goes upstairs. This clipping they will not take back home.

Imam remains in the sitting room, waiting until he can hear the floorboards creaking overhead. From his kurta pocket, he removes the pocket watch he has been keeping on his person ever since it landed at his feet. The silver disk, better than any medal, warms his palm. He draws a fingertip over the engraved lines, each as fine as a feline whisker.

As word spreads of the Lion and the Panther of the Punjab, all the European wrestlers fall silent but one—Stanislaus Zbyszko, the winner of the Greco-Roman world championship tournament at the Casino de Paris four years ago, ranked number one in the world before his more recent scandal with Yousuf the Terrible. This time, Zbyszko is looking to rebuild his name and promises a match with no foul play. He and Gama will face off at the John Bull Tournament in early July.

"This is it," Mr. Benjamin says to Gama. "You pin him, you'll be world champion. *You*—" Here he jabs a finger at Gama's chest. "*Rustom! E! Zamana!*" Mr. Benjamin's pronunciation brings a smile to Gama's face.

Imam is less amused. He detects a growing whiff of greed about Mr. Benjamin in the way he goads Gama toward desire and impatience, the very emotions they have been taught to hold at bay. Just as troubling is his refusal to offer a clear figure of ticket sales, though he promises to give them their earnings in one bulk sum at the end.

Out of habit and innocence, Gama puts his faith in Mr. Benjamin. Through him, Gama dispatches a single message in *Sporting Life:* he will throw the Pole three times in the space of an hour.

Imam has seen pictures of Zbyszko: the fused boulders of muscle, the bald head like the mean end of a battering ram. Even hanging by his sides, his arms are a threat. Gama has seen the pictures too, but they never speak of Zbyszko, or his size, or his titles. They refer only to the match.

News of the bout spreads to India. Mr. Mishra, their Bengali patron, writes Gama a rousing letter, imploring him to prove to the world that "India is not only a land of soft-bodied coolies and clerks." Mishra rhapsodizes over Bharat Mata and her hard-bodied sons, comparing Gama to the Hindu warrior Bhim. Regarding Europeans, Mr. Mishra has only one opinion: "All they know is croquet and crumpets."

Imam isn't sure if Mr. Mishra knows that Zbyszko is a

Pole. He considers writing back, then recalls the article with Dhingra's picture, the words "traitor" and "treason" captioning it. Once, a journalist asked Gama and Imam about their political leanings, whether they considered themselves "moderate" or "radical." Imam turned to Gama, each searching the other for the correct answer, before Gama, bewildered, said, "We are *pehlwan*."

Those words return to Imam later, as he sets a lit match to the letter. They do not want trouble. He holds the burning letter over the sink and then rinses the ash down the drain.

A week remains until the John Bull Tournament. Life narrows its borders, contains only wrestling and meditation, *bethak* and *dand*, *yakhi* and ghee and almonds. Food is fuel, nothing more. They wake at three in the morning and retire at eight in the evening, their backs to the sunset slicing through the crack between the curtains.

For all their time together, Imam has never felt further from his brother. He can detect some deep tidal turn within Gama, a gravity at his core, pulling him inward and inward again into a wordless coil of concentration. He declines all interviews. His gaze is a wall.

Lying in bed, Imam imagines entering the ring with Zbyszko. He pictures himself executing an artful series of moves never witnessed on these shores, the Flying Cobra perhaps, an overhead lift, a twirl and a toss. The papers would remember him all over again. Twitching with energy, he can hardly sleep.

One day, he upends Gama with the Flying Cobra. Imam knows he should withdraw, but something snaps in him, and it happens in a blink: Imam dives and pins his brother.

Imam lies there, wide-eyed, panting. Beneath him is Gama

the Great, *Rustom-e-Hind,* Boy Hero of *Bethaks* with his cheek against the mat. No one has ever pinned him, until now.

"Get up," Gama says.

Imam springs to his feet, embarrassed. He knows better than to offer his brother a hand. Somehow he wants Gama to strike out at him, to rear up in anger or indignation.

Gama sits for a moment, catching his breath, before he hoists himself up and shifts his jaw right and left, back into place.

"Again," Gama says, tugging at his *langot.* "Again."

July arrives and, on a damp evening, the John Bull Tournament. Gama and Imam enter a music hall with cut-out cartoons of clowns between the windows, and a painted lady in a twirling skirt, her knees exposed. Imam does his best to ignore these ivory knees. White lights reading HOLBORN EMPIRE silver the cobbled street below, the stones shining like fish scales.

Inside, the arena smells unpleasantly of wet wool. Mr. Benjamin keeps twisting around in his seat to take in the hundreds of spectators. "Sold out," he enunciates to Imam, turning his hands upward. "No more tickets. None!"

Imam says, "Yes, splendid," unable to remove his gaze from Zbyszko. He stands in the opposite corner of the ring, twisting his torso from side to side. He seems larger than in his pictures, his head so prominent and bald that his ears are reduced to small, pink cups. In the ring, Gama does one *bethak* after another, taking no notice of his opponent.

Finished with *bethaks,* Gama turns his back on Zbyszko and jogs in place, opening and closing his hands. Imam realizes that he is warming up more than usual, as if to keep his mind occupied. The day before, Gama looked up from his chicken broth and said, "I heard he once squeezed a man unconscious."

Imam dismissed this as nonsense, but they said nothing else for several minutes, picturing Zbyszko and his victim, limp as a pelt at his feet.

The bell clangs. Gama lunges, felling Zbyszko with a neat foot hook. He clamps Zbyszko with a half nelson, flings him over, and pins his shoulder to the mat. Zbyszko keeps his other shoulder raised as long as he can, quivering. Imam leans forward, wills the other shoulder to kiss the mat.

But now, a shock: Zbyszko wriggles out of Gama's clutch.

Zbyszko then deploys a move so bizarre that Imam thinks it a practical joke. Without warning, Zbyszko falls to the mat on all fours. Like a farm animal.

Gama tries to push him over or pull him up by the waist, but Zbyszko bears down, muttering as if to brace himself against the hurled curses of the spectators. He will not move. Gama tries the wrist lock, the quarter nelson—every hold he can imagine—but Zbyszko will not be thrown; nor will he attempt a throw.

A tiresome hour passes, for the most part, in deadlock. People bark, pitch insults and peanut hulls, cursing Zybzsko more than Gama, though neither is spared. Imam sits with his hand propped against his mouth, speechless. Even if he could be heard over the din, he wouldn't know what to say.

At one point Gama's hands fall to his sides. He looks helplessly at Imam, who shakes his head.

A crumpled wad of newspaper bounces off Zbyszko's rounded back. Spectators thunder to the exits. The match is eventually stopped, and it is decided that both parties will wrestle again the following Saturday.

·

Imam opens the door to Gama's bedroom. In all the weeks they have been staying in this house, he has never seen his brother's room until now, the day before they are leaving. He enters to find a vast bed, Gama's suitcase lying open upon it. On the nightstand is a glass of water, a few yellow wildflowers wilting over the rim. Imam stares at the sullen blooms, unable to imagine his brother bending to pick them.

Gama gets up suddenly from the window seat, as if caught in a private moment. He asks if Imam has packed.

"I was helping Ahmed," Imam says. "His is the heaviest trunk." The cook brought an endless supply of ghee and almonds, not knowing when they would return.

Imam runs a hand over the oak footboard and peers into the suitcase. Among the clothing, Gama has nested a trio of paper-wrapped soaps for their mother and a tin of Crawford's biscuits in the shape of a barrel organ, with finely painted green wheels and a tiny monkey extending its hat. Mr. Benjamin procured the gifts for them. He has promised to send along their earnings once their bills are settled up, a promise that Gama doesn't care enough about to question.

Wedged in between the gifts is the John Bull belt. Imam holds it up to his face. The leather is soft and pliant, the center plate broad and bordered in gold scrollwork. On the plate is a painting of a heavyset man wearing britches tucked into his boots and a black top hat. This, presumably, is John Bull, and peering from behind his ankles is a bulldog who shares his build. Englishmen and their dogs—Imam will never understand the attraction. There are a great many things he will never understand.

Gama was awarded the belt two days before, after showing up for the rematch only to learn that Zbyszko had fled the country. Gama won by forfeit. Only a handful of people clapped as Gama received the belt from the referee and raised it limply over his head. He never even removed his turban and robe.

The next day, a journalist called the house, wanting a comment on Percy Woodmore's recent opinion in *Health & Strength,* which stated that Gama "showed a surprising ignorance of strategy" in the match against Zbyszko. The journalist also referred to rumors, hinted at in Woodmore's piece, that Zbyszko had secretly agreed to flee the country if Gama paid him a percentage of his winnings. The journalist said, "Hello?" several times before Imam set the phone back on its hook.

Imam replaces the belt and peers around it. "You forgot the newspapers," he says. "Everyone will want to see them."

Gama shakes his head. "There's no room." He shuts and buckles the suitcase. Imam moves to help him, but Gama has already hefted the box in both hands, and eases it onto the floor, next to his battered leather valise.

He smooths down the bedspread and, with his back to Imam, casually asks if the newspapers have said anything about the John Bull Tournament.

"Just the usual nonsense," Imam says.

"But someone called yesterday. You looked upset."

"Oh, what does it matter." Imam squints through the window, as if the sky has claimed all his attention. He can feel his brother's eyes on him. "We are going home."

"You aren't telling me something." When Imam doesn't answer, Gama raises his voice. "I am not a child, Imam."

Imam turns to face his brother, who stands rigid with irritation. "Some are saying that you paid Zbyszko to run away. They say that's how you got the belt."

Gama blinks as this news crashes over him. He takes a step back, his hand fumbling for the edge of the bed before he sits.

He has never looked more like a child, Imam thinks, even when he was a child.

"But who . . . ," Gama begins, then drops his gaze to the floor and does not speak for a long time.

"It's just a rumor," Imam says quickly. "A stupid rumor. Back home, you are a hero." He tells of the telegram that just arrived from Mishra, reporting the top headline from *The Times of India:* GAMA THE GREATEST—INDIA WINS WORLD CHAMPIONSHIP.

Gama gives a weak smile. "Is that what they've decided."

"You have the belt to prove it," Imam says. For a long moment, Gama looks over his shoulder at the suitcase but does not go near it. "It's true—"

"No, *chotu*. I am just a pawn."

He says this so softly he could be talking to himself, if not for that one tender word, which Imam has not heard from him in years. It is as if they are eight and twelve again, and Gama has set him apart from everyone else—*chotu*. Imam feels himself rising to the word. Inglorious as it is, this is something that for once only he can be. Only he knows to say nothing, to rest his hand at the back of his brother's neck, to let his grip say everything, or simply: *Not to me.*

What to Do with Henry

...

Saffa couldn't tell how long the chimpanzee had been hanging by its ankle from the *ndokuwuli* tree. There was a frailty to the thing, suspended but still. The chimpanzee had to be female, judging by the baby huddled directly beneath her, squeaking hoarsely and baring its teeth. Of baby chimpanzees, he had heard that they never left their mothers, dead or alive or hanging by a single limb.

The trap had been set by Saffa's uncle, who owned the surrounding papaya trees and was fed up with marauding monkeys. He had sent Saffa to check the traps that morning, and at the time, Saffa was pleased to be dispatched on what he considered a man's errand. He was seventeen, and when his father's friends came by the house, they still sent him to the kiosk to bring them back cold drinks, as though he were a boy. If only he were on his bicycle right now, rather than here, a rack of bottled beers clinking in his wire basket.

Saffa glanced at the long, curled toes. According to the paramount chief, he wasn't supposed to set eyes on a dead

chimpanzee, let alone kill it; the chimpanzee was a sacred animal, like the leopard and the bush cow, off-limits to hunters
and farmers. But now what? He might have turned away and
headed home and made himself forget everything were it not
for the baby.

Saffa gathered the baby into his large, awkward hands, its
terror reverberating through his palms. Its head was smaller
than a mango, and its eyes were liquid and searching. He felt
sorry for the orphaned thing, but ah!—a flash of hope. He
knew exactly what to do with it.

He took the baby chimp to Nguebu Market. Sometimes Peace
Corps people drifted through the market, their gazes casting about for souvenirs; they were known to pay high prices
for baby chimps, which they liked to keep as pets. The Peace
Corps people were built of a mystifying courage that made
them unafraid of the animals those babies would become one
day, wild and possessed of the strength of five men.

Saffa set up a stool beside the other vendors who lined Mahei
Boima Road, which was so choked with commerce that hardly
a bicycle could pass. People forged their way through on foot:
a woman with a plate of pineapple on her head, a boy with a
tower of twelve plastic buckets balanced on his own. Saffa put
the baby in a cardboard box and waited. He tried to appear
cool against the questioning eyes of the vendors, tried to ignore
the mewling sound that the baby had begun to make. He fixed
a careless gaze on the rice seller across from him, whose own
baby straddled her back within a red wrap, perhaps the same
placid position in which the baby chimp had been before its
mother took one wrong step and flew into the sky.

A half hour later, a pair of tourists made their way down the road, a white woman behind sunglasses and a golden little girl in a frothy Western dress, with the dark braids of a local. The little girl held the white woman's hand and trailed behind. He watched their twined fingers, the dark and light of them.

The white woman stopped before the cardboard box. In her, Saffa saw the yawning unhappiness of rich people, a kind of boredom with life that had brought her here, along with so many other tourists, to give color to her life. But Saffa did not fawn and pander like the handicraft people when they dealt with tourists. He remained on the stool, pinching the calluses at the base of his fingers.

When the white woman peered into the box, the baby chimp raised its hands to her. Saffa said, "He want you to carry him."

The woman glanced at Saffa, obviously surprised that he knew English. She had no idea that he had been the smartest of his form-five class, that he had taught himself English from movies. He spoke a few words of Krio to the little girl, which made her smile. Somewhat relaxed, the woman picked up the baby chimp, and it sat quietly in the crook of her arm.

He could see how human the chimp looked to the white woman. The color of its face was nearly as pink as her own, though most likely its skin would later darken like its mother's. Saffa did not mention the mother. He said that he had found the baby in a forest, abandoned.

Not only did Saffa know English words; he also knew English numbers, and refused to go below thirty-five dollars for the chimp. After paying him, the white woman removed the shawl from her shoulders and wrapped the baby inside it, oblivious to those who stared at her. She took the little girl by the hand, and together they made their way through the crowd. Saffa watched this strange little trio, pleased by the sale and yet reluctant to look away, curious as to what would become of them.

. . .

The woman who bought the chimpanzee was named Pearl Groves, and she was no idiot. She could smell the lies rolling off that poacher as strongly as his sweat, a nose for deceit that she'd acquired much too late in her marriage.

Pearl's husband was a noted herpetologist who had visited western Cameroon in 1969 to research the Hairy Frog, *Trichobatrachus robustus,* whose males were not in fact hairy but covered with tiny, cilia-like extensions of skin, allowing them more surface area through which to breathe. His love affair with the Hairy Frog had lasted for months, permeating their breakfast conversation and even surfacing, embarrassingly, at some dinner parties. Pearl found it hard to be inquisitive on the subject. She had never shared her husband's love for amphibians but contented herself with the idea that their marriage was like a frozen dinner, compartmentalized but complementary.

Six years after her husband ended his research trips, a letter followed. Pearl was gentle with the paper, torn along one corner, as fragile and baffling as a salvaged treasure map. The letter was written by an NGO worker in Sierra Leone, on behalf of an old woman whose daughter had died of malaria, leaving her with a granddaughter whose education and care she could not shoulder. Along with the letter came a small black-and-white photograph of a child with the eyes and dimples and mouth of Pearl's husband. On the back of the photograph was written: *Neneh, daughter of Mr. Groves.*

Pearl was sixty years old, a retired schoolteacher who had never wanted children. Neither had her husband. People assumed that this was because Pearl considered her students her children, a pleasant lie to which she sometimes resorted, but in reality, she couldn't see how children fit into the frozen dinner of her marriage. And as far as an extramarital affair was concerned, she had presumed that her husband had passed the window of foolish opportunity. A part of her eyed him with wonder, searching for the rogue within, the simmering of lust. But at sixty-four, he had a belly that sagged over his belt; he mumbled nonsense in his sleep. Sometimes, if he was especially riveted by *The $10,000 Pyramid* while brushing his teeth, he would continue to brush, like a machine, until the foam streamed down his chin as he yelled, "Things that bite! THINGS THAT BITE!" And now, reading and rereading the letter, she kept wondering if it all would have been different had she just gone to Cameroon with her husband, had she just pretended to love those disgusting frogs.

Maybe then he would have left his cleaning woman alone. The woman was originally from Bo, her husband admitted, haltingly. Sierra Leone. She had been new to Cameroon, like him, and lonely.

Everyone in Pearl's family implored her to come to her senses; one did not leave her home in Canton, Ohio, to retrieve a girl from a hut in Africa. Send money their way and be done with it. This was her husband's view as well, though he had lost most of his authority and his life had become a prolonged exercise in deference: submitting the TV remote to Pearl, making a tuna melt for Pearl, shuffling out of any room she entered. Pearl simply replied that adopting Neneh was the right thing to do, leaning upon the brand of Baptist conviction that had always sustained her. Behind that conviction was her intention to shame her husband every day, to raise the mirror to his face and show him she was not deceived; she knew exactly who he was.

Pearl's husband thought her insane for going to Sierra Leone. He refused to accompany her or take her to the airport. She left him the number of the hotel in Bo where she and Neneh would be staying for a week, preparing for the flight back home. Whenever he tried to change the subject, Pearl switched it right back. Whenever he grudgingly referred to "the girl," Pearl asserted her name—*Neneh*.

But when Pearl arrived in Bo to claim Neneh, all her stern conviction dissolved, displaced by the immediate necessities of the child made real. Because Neneh's grandmother was too old to travel from her village, Neneh had come with a representative from the NGO, a plumpish woman wearing a head wrap of blue and green and a matching skirt that fishtailed around her ankles. They had dinner in the hotel restaurant, groundnut soup and country rice, while the woman talked about Neneh's mother. Pearl had thought that learning of the other woman would crush her, but instead she was oddly fascinated. Isatu had taken any number of jobs to support her child, selling cassava by the road and dyeing *gara* fabrics. The NGO worker kept saying the word "suffer" over and over: "Even just for buy half back and feeding and clothing, she suffered *a lot*." The whole time, Pearl was vaguely aware of Neneh regarding her with a strange vigilance, as if trying to memorize her entirely.

When it was time for the NGO woman to leave, she kissed Neneh once on each cheek and accepted the package Pearl had brought for Neneh's grandmother, gifts that seemed all wrong. What would the old woman do with a flannel nightgown in this broiling heat? Pearl had also slipped money up the nightgown's sleeve, but would Neneh's grandmother know where to convert the dollar bills?

For Neneh, Pearl had brought a red headband and a lacy white dress that would surely attract swarms of sienna dust. Dutifully, Neneh fit the headband over her braids and refused to remove it until she went to bed. With equal resolve, she would not go anywhere without holding Pearl's hand. While Neneh slept, Pearl stared at the girl's curled fingers, her hard palm inscribed with the same lines that appeared on her father's. The lines filled Pearl with wonder rather than hate, and it was at that moment, tracing the birdlike bones of Neneh's hand, that Pearl understood how hate could carry her only so far.

Several days before they left for Ohio, Pearl thought it would be good to get Neneh out of the hotel. Pearl had chosen the hotel for its royal-sounding name—Sir Milton—but the toilet bowl was bereft of its seat, the water tasted of metal, and the mosquito nets had holes that left her scratching all night. The receptionist suggested that they visit the Cotton Tree, the site where the first African-American slaves, freed and arrived in 1792, had held a thanksgiving mass. Pearl felt apathetic about visiting a tree, but it turned out to be more astonishing, more alive than any monument she had seen, its massive trunk roped and coiled with fantastical vines as thick as her arm, with bat-filled branches that sprawled up against the pale blue sky. Deriving some strength from its ancient shade, Pearl felt that she could stand and stare forever at the tree, with Neneh at her side, and for the first time during her visit, she felt capable of everything her friends and family had dismissed.

When she and Neneh walked past the vendors, Pearl did not flinch at what she saw: the dismembered parts of what seemed to be a goat, lying in the heat, bright with blood; the stares of local children gleefully pointing at her and calling out, *"Pumui! Pumui!"* There were women selling fruits and vegetables piled on burlap, green plantains and thick fingers of cassava, tables of trinkets in bowls, balls of black soap, mountains of country and white rice, hills of sesame seeds and black-eyed peas. Toward the end of their walk, Pearl and Neneh came upon a baby chimpanzee in a cardboard box.

As Pearl reached for the chimp, she felt a rejuvenating sense of certainty, a rectitude with no moral or rational ground. She was destroying her old life, blow by blow, and building a new one out of new names. Neneh, and now *Henry;* the name came to Pearl as a breeze. She tucked Henry into her orange shawl and stroked the soft saucers of his ears. She did not consider what her husband would think of this latest development. It didn't matter. He hadn't called a single time, and Pearl had known all along that he would not be home when she returned.

• • •

On the plane, Henry was so wide-eyed and serene that the flight attendants let him ride in Pearl's lap, swaddled in her shawl. It had been relatively easy for Pearl to secure the import and export permits necessary for his adoption, but later that year, the United States issued a ban on the importation of chimpanzees as pets, citing them as health hazards and possible vessels for disease. Pearl was relieved that Henry had slipped by the ban. She dismissed the thought that her little coconut could be a hazard to anyone.

So for a time, there was Pearl, Neneh, and Henry. In Canton, Henry adapted well to their lives, eating at the dinner table and watching television in earnest, especially if a nature documentary appeared on PBS. He enjoyed simple pleasures— a fried egg sandwich, a Dole fruit cup, the dial tone of an unhooked phone. Pearl grew so frustrated with finding phones off the hook that she gripped Henry by the arm and scolded him; he avoided her eyes. After she released him and sat down to watch the evening news, he leapt into her lap and planted an open-mouthed kiss on her lips.

Those were difficult years, when most of Pearl's friends and family stopped visiting, their phone calls dwindling. Pearl made them uncomfortable. Once, in her mailbox, she found a folded drawing of herself as a chimp, with a sloping forehead, flaring nostrils, a bun. She'd had smart-ass students before, but this somehow made her face simmer with shame. She rolled up the paper and used it to twirl out the spiderwebs inside the mailbox.

Pearl forged ahead. She took it upon herself to homeschool Neneh in all subjects, well through the fourth grade. Neneh was a poor student, and sometimes Pearl wondered if she was progressing sluggishly on purpose, reluctant to join a school with children her own age.

When Neneh turned ten years old, she enrolled at Walden Middle School, a short bus ride away. On the second day of class, Jurgen Roberts turned to her and asked, "Is it true your brother's a chimp?" Just as Neneh was about to answer, Miss Davis demanded to know why Jurgen would ever say such a thing about someone's brother.

Neneh left school that day with the distinct impression that the answer she had almost given Jurgen Roberts was wrong. The correct answer to his question would have been: *Henry's not my brother, he's my pet.* She considered treating Henry as she had seen other people dealing with their dogs and cats, as though she were an authority whose job it was to tame his behaviors. One such behavior was his proclivity to blow kisses at the blond mailwoman who slipped their mail through the slot and blew him a kiss in return. It was weird. What if, by some slim and lovely chance, Natalie Sharpe came over to play one day? Would Henry, beguiled by her flaxen hair, try to kiss her, too?

But Natalie Sharpe moved to Indiana, and Jurgen Roberts started going with Allie Sanfilippo, the girl who sat in front of him, at which point he stopped turning his head farther than forty-five degrees. Everything about the world of school was mercurial, the alliances tenuous, the cafeteria a minefield; at home, Henry was always waiting for her on the foyer stairs. He was her brother, whose leathery soles she liked to tickle until he gave desperate, panting bursts of laughter. A brother who winced when the trunk door fell on her head, who rubbed his own head in sympathy. A brother who stole the last grape Popsicle before she'd had even one, but at the very least, if she complained, he would break off a melty half and hold it out to her on his palm. "The half with the stick," Neneh would insist, and, playing innocent, he would look away, as if he couldn't understand her.

Seven years later, Pearl was forced to donate Henry to a zoo. The county police department had been pressuring her to do so, ever since Pearl's neighbor had informed the sheriff that Pearl was harboring an adult male chimpanzee, who, if angered, could lash out with savage strength. It didn't matter when Neneh and Pearl tried to explain Henry's many gentle aspects, how patient he was, how delighted by buttered popcorn, so much so that he stood rapt before the microwave, watching the flat envelope spin in the humming light, growing pregnant with his favorite food. He even knew how to press the Minute-Plus button, as well as Start and Open.

"Popcorn?" the sheriff said, as if to imply that Pearl was choosing popcorn over local security.

But gradually it became difficult for Pearl to ignore that she was aging. Her veins rose blue against her thinning skin, and various glands and muscles made her wake with a start in the night. She was seventy-two years old and Neneh was seventeen, too young to care for a fully grown chimp on her own.

After many disappointing zoo tours, Pearl gave her reluctant approval to the Willow Park Zoo, in Florida, which provided a wider sanctuary than the primate pens she had seen, where the chimps were often numb with depression and boredom, butting their heads against the walls of their cages or masturbating. Here, the chimpanzee enclosure appeared larger, almost the size of a gymnasium, with a multitude of trees, both live and dead, and a flaccid waterfall between knobby gray boulders. Some chimpanzees were busy grooming each other, others explored the underbellies of stones they had doubtless explored before, while the younger ones tickled and tumbled around one another. It seemed to Pearl the best she could do.

The zoo curator was eager to adopt Henry, as the zoo had no adult male chimpanzees and, thus, no way of breeding. Pearl refused any payment in return but was adamant in her negotiations: (1) that she and Neneh be allowed to privately visit with Henry, and (2) that Henry not be traded or sold. Papers were signed and promises made; Henry was brought to the zoo.

Upon first hearing the shrieks of his new family, Henry scrambled up to the roof of the cafeteria, his mouth stretched into a fear grin, all teeth and pink gums. Neneh coaxed him down, offering him a Dole fruit cup, while Pearl made kissing noises. She raised her hands to him. Eventually, he descended, but he continued yelping while Neneh and Pearl took turns embracing him. His legs were quivering.

Pearl paid no attention to the keepers and the curator who stood around, hands on their hips, exchanging worried glances. Pearl murmured softly but firmly to Henry, which was what she used to do when thunderstorms drove him out of his own bed and into her arms. She did her very best to comfort him, without crooning or condescending as though he were a baby or a dog, as much for Henry's sake as for these keepers. She wanted them to know that Henry should be treated with as much dignity as they would afford to each other, and that he was as precious to her as any human being who had walked into or out of her life.

. . .

At the zoo, the female chimps despised Henry. The keepers had no idea what to do. Without support from a single female, Henry had no chance of melding with the group, let alone achieving the rank of alpha male.

There were four adult females plus Max, a baby boy. As the oldest female, Nana had taken up the position of alpha male, and though Henry made no effort to seize power, his very presence posed a challenge to her reign. Each morning during the first week, as soon as the chimps were released from their night cages, Nana and her gang of disgruntled females went after Henry in a screaming blitzkrieg that didn't cease until he had been chased into the upper reaches of a tree. Sometimes Nana bit at his feet and drew blood, her allies screeching at Henry from below. Henry's legs shook; he vomited. Nothing he ate stayed down for long anyway, owing to his preference for omelets and sausage over the zoo's food pellets.

Joseph, the oldest keeper, felt for Henry. He remembered how Mrs. Groves had held Henry before she'd left. The way she'd cupped the crown of his head was not unlike the way Joseph's sister Julia had cradled her son's, though Chip was eighteen years old and lying in a casket. Drunk, he had sped his mother's car across a patch of black ice and into a tree. Now his photographs were used in the drunk-driving videos shown to high schoolers and DUI offenders, a picture of Chip, pale and unprepared for the flash, and next to this, his Civic like a crumple of metal Kleenex. These thoughts had been fresh in Joseph's mind as he'd offered Mrs. Groves his handkerchief. She had hesitated before taking it. After blotting her eyes, she'd said, "Thank you," and pulled herself straight.

At Joseph's suggestion, the keepers removed Nana from the sanctuary and kept her in separate quarters for a week. By the time she returned, the other females had grown used to Henry, who most enjoyed playing with little Max. The females had even begun to greet Henry as they would the alpha male, grunting before him as they lowered themselves onto their knuckles, as if doing quick push-ups. Joseph wondered how Henry knew to sit up tall before the bowing female, how he knew to bristle his coat so that he appeared larger than all the others. Whether from memory or instinct, Henry seemed to understand that he could gain authority from these daily greetings.

When finally Nana returned to the group, she chased Henry into a tree, but none of the other females joined her. The next day, Henry retaliated by staying his ground, bristling his coat and baring the dagger-sized canines that she lacked. When Nana growled at him, he slapped her across the face so hard that she fell and rolled onto her side. Screaming in protest, she fled to the other females, who embraced her and calmed her, but did not defend her.

•

Over the next ten years, keepers came and went. A Bengal tiger died after a visitor threw it a fudge brownie that had been sugared with ground glass. The zoo curator was fired, replaced by a woman intent on raising more money. The new curator used the negative publicity to hold a fund-raiser, which supplied the budget to enlarge several quarters so that animals were now kept at a greater distance from the visitors, behind a transparent plastic shield.

The shield proved frustrating for Henry, who was used to flirting in close proximity to blond women. Before, when a blonde would peer at the cage from behind the hip-high visitor bar, Henry would hoist himself onto the rock closest to her and blow kisses. He'd then drop to his hands and began swaying back and forth, his fur ruffled, ready to mate.

The visitors were amused by the spectacle, especially the blondes, who were happy to play Fay Wray and blow kisses in return, until they noticed his erection, and recoiled. It was no game to Henry. Rejected, he wandered away from the blondes to sit on a distant stone.

His attraction to blondes rendered him completely uninterested in females of his own kind. He refused to mate with any female chimp, even when she offered herself in times of estrus, the brief window in which she was willing. He kept at a distance, scrutinizing his nails or searching the sky. The youngest female, Gigi, became so enamored of Henry that when he didn't respond, she would run up, thrust a hand between his legs, and try to manually raise his interest. This only provoked him to move away, at which point Gigi would throw herself to the ground, screaming until Max came along.

Max was now entering his adolescence and eager for every opportunity among the females. But unlike most alpha males,

Henry did not grow jealous when Max mated with another female; nor did Henry exercise his dominance by disrupting the couple and chasing Max away. Ever the gentleman, and possibly relieved, Henry looked the other way as yet another orgasmic shriek split the sky.

"Give him time," Joseph told the perplexed curator. "He might be depressed. Or gay." The smile slid off her face.

Joseph sensed a long-steeping sadness in Henry, dark as his own. His girlfriend had been trying to snap him out of it. Elaine had even taken to stitching ugly pillows with Bible verses, and he loved each wobbly seam. He loved her, too, but he wondered when she would leave him. Joseph could tell that she was tiring of him, especially since he had refused to seek the services of a pastor or a shrink. He couldn't help his beliefs—namely, that there was very little to believe in, though he did believe in Henry's right to withdraw from females if he felt like it, to withdraw from the whole world when it seemed too harsh to weather. Sometimes it was a wonder that more people were not huddled like Henry, praying for life to pass quietly.

But in time, after the glass shield was erected, Gigi prevailed upon Henry. The keepers were unsure of when and how exactly this happened, but Joseph was the first to notice Henry mounting Gigi on a tranquil Saturday afternoon, without excitement or energy, simply because it seemed required of him. The act inspired a variety of responses among the zoo visitors. Some snickered and laughed; others primly turned away. As for Joseph, he sensed Henry's sadness and surrender. On some occasions, Henry continued to court the blondes, even if from a distance, even if their rejections led him to perch among the branches of a dead oak and sullenly watch the clouds.

• • •

Henry was in his early twenties when a new volunteer joined the Willow Park staff, and at first, no one recognized her. Only Joseph, the oldest keeper still in employment, squinted at her in the sunlight and asked, "Aren't you the Groves girl?"

Neneh smiled through her headache, caused by the red headband cinching her close-cropped hair. At twenty-seven, she was probably too old to be wearing a headband. At least that was what Pearl would have said, as she believed in "dressing your age, not the age you want to be." In her last days, Pearl always wore her antique pearl-drop earrings, even to sleep, even to her grave.

Only a few people had attended the funeral the month before. Pearl had been sick for years, and over time, she'd withdrawn from her remaining friends and kept to the house. Toward the end, there were many nights when she tossed in her sleep, calling out for Henry until Neneh crept into bed and held her.

Pearl hadn't spoken his name in years. She had refused to visit Henry, in spite of the contract; nor would she allow Neneh to do so, believing that he would survive among his fellow chimps only if he forgot his old life, his more human behaviors. "He can't be two things at once," she said, to which Neneh wanted to ask, *Why not?* But Neneh said nothing, knowing that Pearl also wanted to forget Henry, and the family they had been.

While in high school, Neneh found an article about Henry in a Florida newspaper, titled "The Ape Who Loved Blondes over Baboons." She didn't show it to Pearl.

Several years later, Pearl's kidney began to fail. Neneh decided to live at home throughout college, to watch over Pearl. She accompanied Pearl on her thrice-weekly trips to the hospital, where Pearl was attached to a dishwasher of a machine that cleansed her blood and sent it back into her forearm. When they finally got the letter that a kidney was available, Neneh baked a kidney-shaped red velvet cake. "Ugly and damn good," Pearl declared with a red velvet grin, and suddenly it seemed to Neneh that everything would be fine.

But soon after the operation, Pearl's body began to refuse the new kidney. Her face swelled from the antirejection drugs; her limbs dwindled. Neneh could feel her own body humming with terror and energy. Whenever the hospice nurse tried to take Neneh aside and carefully talk about Pearl's hypertension, "a bad sign," Neneh bit at her fingernails so intently that all she heard was the sound of her clicking teeth. When Pearl began to murmur of funeral arrangements, Neneh went in search of fluffier pillows. Neneh made every effort to be of use, to pave the way toward Pearl's decline with petals and prayers, as if death were a graceful thing, not the gradual gouging of life from Pearl's eyes until what was left was only a decimating, and yet ordinary, stillness.

And now, here she was, at the Willow Park Zoo, a place she had longed for ever since she left it.

"How is your grandmother?" Joseph asked.

"She's fine, just too old to travel."

Neneh hadn't planned on lying, but the truth would have led Joseph to treat her as everyone did, with equal portions of care and discomfort. Neneh knew how she was often perceived: a girl who had revolved around Pearl for decades and now, having no one else, was a planet spinning out into the unknown.

But as strong as her pull toward Pearl had been, Neneh had always felt an equal pull in Henry's direction. She had done her college thesis on "Cooperative Behavior Among Captive

Chimpanzees"; she had kept the newspaper clipping about Henry and the blondes; she had brought along the contract with the Willow Park Zoo. She could not have admitted it to herself when Pearl was alive, but as the end approached, Neneh had felt a small and terrible part of her waiting to be released.

. . .

Nervous about seeing Henry, Neneh wandered the grounds on her first day at the zoo. Many animals were new to her, like the antlered blesbok behind rusted grids of wire and the Chilean flamingos with their knotted knees. She meandered through the Bird Hut, filled with the soft hiss and squeak of the Balinese mynah, the toucan, and the fruit dove, mingled with the noise of stroller wheels and shouting children, disappointedly searching the cages.

Eventually, Neneh made her way through the Primate Forest, past the red-nosed mandrills and the goateed colobus monkeys, finally arriving at the chimp enclosure. A zoo worker named Britta was sitting on the bench in front of the enclosure, a pretty face if not for the poorly dyed orange blond of her hair. She seemed to know a great deal about the different chimpanzees, their alliances, their diets, their "mouth-mouth contact." Neneh searched the enclosure, unsuccessfully, for a face she recognized.

Britta pointed out Henry, who was crouched before a termite mound, a stick in his fist, which he dipped into the mound to fish for termites. He looked darker and rangier than Neneh had expected, especially compared to Max, whom Britta called "the new alpha male." Max's thick, bristly hair was being groomed by one of the females while Henry sat alone. Neneh searched Henry's face, but she was too far away to tell whether his eyes were still the hue of maple syrup. She waited for him to look up and notice the red headband she was wearing, which she had bought from a department store back in Canton, thinking that this might jog his memory to the first time they'd met in Bo. But he did not look up from his termite mound.

Britta explained last month's upheaval, how Max had overthrown Henry through a mounting assault of bluff displays, which often ended in blows. Over the years, Max had grown to be Henry's physical equal, and by nature Max was confrontational, often violent. Once, during a more brutal fight, Max tore a gash across the sole of Henry's foot so that Henry limped for days. Presuming that this was a game, two of the newer children, Crouch and Walt, followed Henry in a single-file line, mimicking his limp.

As Britta chattered on, Neneh felt a thickening knot in her throat. "But no one stepped in to help Henry?" she demanded.

"Well, we can't butt in whenever we want," Britta said tautly. Neneh looked out at the man-made boulders, the man-made trickle of water between them. "We can't just impose our world on theirs. Chimpanzees abide by their own rules, even if they're in captivity."

At that moment, Henry looked up. Neneh sat perfectly still. She imagined his world and her world, two distinct, delicate bubbles floating toward each other, hovering as he fixed her with his faraway gaze. Did he see the red headband? Did he recognize her voice?

He dropped his eyes and went back to poking the ground.

For that week, Neneh rented a room at the Motor Inn, which came equipped with a hot plate, a coffeepot, an iron, and a mirror that took up the entire wall opposite the bed. With the blue-green wallpaper and drawn shades, the room had a contained, nautical feel.

Here, she ruminated over Britta's words, the note of accusation when she'd said "impose our world." It was the same accusation Pearl had inflicted upon herself ever since leaving Henry at the zoo. By rescuing him, they had ruined him.

Sometimes Neneh wondered if Pearl had felt similarly about rescuing her. Pearl had never tried to contact Neneh's relatives in Bo, and gradually Sierra Leone had come to seem to Neneh like yet another photograph in *National Geographic,* the natives serene and strange, the land lush and yet unyielding of its mysteries. With or without Pearl, Neneh would never visit Sierra Leone. Her birth mother was dead, and her grandmother had died soon after she'd left. Strangely, the only face that remained in her mind's eye, like an icon, belonged to the boy who'd sold them baby Henry. She remembered the high, delicate bones of his cheeks, the sweatless sheen of his skin, but he would certainly never remember her. Maybe he was dead as well, or disfigured, or handless, another casualty in a war that was mentioned only marginally in their local paper. Neneh had sought out other newspapers, had read articles that displayed pictures of bandaged limbs and hard-eyed children holding guns. She had been spared.

In college, she had dated a boy, Carl, whose mother was black and whose father was white, both of them from Atlanta. He was proud of his parents' union, forged at a time when some states still declared such intermixing illegal. He kept their picture in his desk drawer, his mother in a sleeveless white dress, bright against her smooth shoulders, smearing cake across her new husband's mouth.

As for Neneh and Carl, the relationship ended in a matter of months. Neneh rarely spent a night away from Pearl, and evetually Carl started dating an Iranian girl who lived down the hall. "She's chill about things," Carl told Neneh. "She gets me."

"Really? Even though she's not your tribe?" *Our tribe* was a phrase that Carl had coined, referring to the racial kinship he shared with Neneh, their twinned experience. Whatever that meant. She would've given anything to have a single picture like the one in his desk, a captured second of ordinary love from the people who made her. Or maybe just her mother. What she had was her own reflection, which told her nothing.

So Neneh had come to the zoo without a plan, with only the belief that, at the very least, she had Henry. As a child, she had felt unrestrained around him, able to breathe freely, at ease with her place in the world. And despite the intervening years, she had come to believe that she shared more with him than with anyone else. They were two ruined souls doomed to wander their minds, if not the earth, trying to remember from whence they came.

Some of the keepers expressed concern over the fact that Neneh would have direct contact with an adult male chimpanzee. Neneh argued that she wanted only to interact with Henry, away from the other chimps; it was a demand that had to be met according to the contract Pearl had signed long ago.

The first reunion was arranged for the afternoon. A keeper named Ben called Henry into the cages while the other chimps remained outside. When Henry entered the cage, his eyes went to the Dole fruit cup, still sealed, sitting close to the bars of the opposite wall. Neneh was kneeling on the other side. Henry no longer moved with a limp, but it seemed to her that his spirit had atrophied, sucked from his frame. She wondered if he thought he was being punished. She raised her hand and waved, a gesture he used to mirror, but now did not.

"Looks like he's in one of his moods," Ben said. He tugged at the bill of his baseball cap and gazed at Henry with disinterest. "No one can talk him out of a funk."

Neneh kept insisting on her privacy, so Ben moved away to sweep an empty cage within shouting distance. "Just don't get too comfy with him. He's still a wild animal. He might not remember old friends."

She turned back to Henry, worried that he had detected the irritation in her voice, but he was avoiding her eyes in favor of the fruit cup. He seemed not to recognize her, despite the red headband, and for a time, there was only the scrape of Ben's broom.

Henry took up the fruit cup. His fingers, long and slim and thick-knuckled, moved with all the care and precision of an old man's, as if the object might jump from his hands if he didn't handle it deliberately. He found the peel-back flap on the lid and opened it as Pearl had taught him to do, an act so perfect, so familiar, that Neneh had trouble containing her smile behind her hand. He drank the syrup first, and she almost laughed when he scooped out a yellow wedge of pineapple with a single finger; Henry always mined the pineapples first. Without hesitation, she reached an open palm through the bars, just as she used to do when asking him to share. Henry put down the fruit cup and watched her hand coming toward him.

With a lunge, he took hold of her wrist so quickly she almost cried out. His grip was frightening in its power and assurance; her bones and tendons were no more than flower stems in his fist.

"Henry, stop," she said quietly, "it's me . . ." But his lips remained sealed, his gaze cold and impassive. Was this the same face that had winced when the trunk door fell on her head? And didn't he rub his crown just as she rubbed her own? She had collected those memories like precious stones, kept them all these years. Hadn't he?

But his grip did not tighten or loosen, and she began to wonder if he was holding her there for a reason. Perhaps he was testing her, to see whether he could trust her as before, or whether she feared him and would squirm free of his clasp. She made herself as still as possible. She flexed her forearm and closed her fist as if to transmit her steadiness, her strength, the solid resolve of a promise, until a distant yell came bearing down on them both: "Henry, let go! . . . *NO, HENRY, NO!*"

Ben rapped his broomstick against the bars. Henry flinched but didn't let go until Ben whacked the bars again, harder this time. Shrieking, Henry scrabbled across the cage to the farthest wall. "Wait," Neneh said, almost to herself, and before she realized what she was doing, she had sprung up and wrenched the broomstick from Ben's hands.

"What the hell," he began to say, but stopped short, silenced by her wild, rage-reddened face.

"Leave him alone," she said hoarsely, in a low, raw voice, as if she'd been shouting for days, years. Ben stood there, staring. "Just leave us the fuck alone!"

Ben backed away, palms raised. "Okay. I'm leaving."

Dropping the broom, she fell to her knees by the cage and reached her arm through the bars, calling to Henry, coaxing, begging even. No matter how she beckoned, Henry would not come. He had turned away from her, a watery blur of black, and all she could do was trace the air with her finger, the question mark curve of his spine.

Somewhere, behind her, Ben was muttering into his walkie-talkie. She knew they wouldn't let her return. She wrapped her hands around the bars and held fast to the only thing that could keep her intact, the remembrance of last night's dream, wherein Henry was being chased by the hunter. Neneh had thrown herself between Henry and the barrel of the hunter's gun, but she felt no pain as the bullet entered her, only an electric tide that swept through her body. This was death—a last, luminous surge. The hunter was gone, but her death was prolonged, painless, as Henry crouched beside her. And though he could not talk, they were communicating in a wordless language all their own, and he was thanking her, he was telling her that he loved her, he was promising her that she was not alone.

The Gulf

...

In later years I will come to avoid him, but for now, I am eight years old, and the man everyone says is my father is sitting in the living room. I watch him, discreetly, from the doorway. He is wearing my mother's baby-blue robe and matching slippers whose seams are pulling apart around his big toe. He arrived the week before with three Air India tags on his single suitcase, looking little like the man in the photograph my mother kept tucked against Psalm 23 of her Bible. In the photo, he was leaning against a coconut tree, an inch of ash on the end of his cigarette.

This was the father I thought we would collect from the airport a week ago. On the morning of his arrival, my mother slipped into her churchgoing heels and dusted her face with Chantilly instead of talcum powder. The Chantilly came in a round pink case as wide as my mother's hand, and inside was a satin pillow that smelled like the type of lady I was almost sure I would someday become. She looked perfect all the way to the airport, until she parked the car and applied a rash of blush to each cheek. "Is it too much?" she asked me, and for the first time in my life, I pitied my mother enough to lie and say no.

"Don't ask him about Dubai," she said. She clapped her compact shut.

But what else would I ask him about? For the past four years my father had been working in the Gulf under a man we called The Sheikh. To me, The Sheikh was a villain robed in black who kept dragging out the work contract by withholding my father's passport. I pictured my father pleading with The Sheikh for a brief vacation, just to spend a few days with my mother and me. I pictured The Sheikh, petting his beard, shaking his head no.

My mother and I were living in Trivandrum when my father left to find work in Dubai, before I could form a memory of him. My friends with fathers didn't treat me differently until the school talent program or my Holy Communion, which all the fathers attended but mine, and suddenly I wasn't myself anymore. I was his absence. Even in my new white veil and black patent shoes, I was the dented suitcase he had left behind, the one with no wheels.

As I grew older, my father remained ageless, preserved by prayers and photos handled only around the edges, and stories whispered by my cousins on rain-battered nights. They said it happened all the time, the men and women who left for the Gulf and never returned, their fates in the hands of cruel Arab employers, their portraits gathering dust on the wall, not even a headstone to hold their places in heaven.

While my father was trapped in the Gulf, my mother wrote on his behalf to consulates, embassies, connections of all kinds until, one day, she received a letter from him that she wouldn't read aloud, not even to her sisters. They stayed up late with her in well-guarded talk, all of them in their mother's enormous barge of a bed, which was actually two beds pushed together and draped with a quilt to hide the crack where I sometimes got wedged in the middle of the night. That night, I didn't belong in the bed or anywhere near it. I could glean only this much: my father was not coming back. No one mentioned him for months. My mother grew hard in some buried way, gained weight. I never saw her eating, but sometimes she would come home with a sweet, sticky hunk of *aluva* wrapped in waxed paper, and not three days later, I would find the waxed paper in the trash.

By year's end, my mother had received a visa to the States, to work as a nurse at a veterans hospital in Baltimore. We moved into a small apartment with rough orange carpeting that had likely seen legions of feet. I had my own room but slept in my mother's bed.

During the days, she left me with the elderly lady down the hall, who insisted that I call her by her first name. We settled on Harriet Auntie. She stunned me with her generosity—a gold tin of chocolates, an Easter basket, a baby doll that drank water through one hole and made water through another. When I showed my mother the doll, she said that if I liked cleaning up pee so much, I could have her job.

Early in the following year, we received a phone call from my father. "He's coming," my mother said, carefully placing the phone in its cradle. I waited for her to weep or laugh or smile, but she kept her hand on the phone, staring at it as if it might spring to life. I knew better than to ask her for specifics, but I imagined a heroic and mysterious escape that included hot words of confrontation, a raised fist, a blackened eye, and a passport produced from the dark tunnel of The Sheikh's sleeve.

.

The man we collected from the airport, the man sitting in the living room, is not the heroic type. He is thinner than in the photos, with coffee-glazed teeth and shoulders that slope like a worn wire hanger. His shirts are lined with a burnt odor that my mother can't get out, no matter how many times she pulls the trigger of her OxiClean.

Aside from the first time he saw me and kissed the top of my head, he hasn't once moved to hug me, as other fathers do. He almost seems afraid of touching my mother, who has stopped with the heels and the blush. Once, we all ate dinner while watching a white family eat dinner on television. Those white people had so much to talk about that the food never even arrived at their mouths. The mother said things like *How was your day?* and *Want seconds?* My father took seconds from a bottle of Jameson.

But this evening, I have caught him alone in the living room, his slippered feet on the coffee table. His eyes are closed, furrows across his forehead, a glass of whiskey in his fist.

I go closer. His fingernails appear recently trimmed, maybe bitten away in that far-off country where he welded metals by day and worried by night. I can just make out the faint freckles across his nose, like a handful of birdseed, the same freckles that appear across my nose every summer.

His eyelashes all of a sudden flutter open. His lips part, releasing a gust of whiskey.

"You're breathing on me," he rasps.

I stop breathing altogether.

His lips widen into a smile I've never seen from him. "I'm just playing, *molay*. Were you afraid?"

"No."

"You're too uptight." He extends his glass to me. "Here, have a little sip."

I take the glass with one hand and drink from the opposite

side of where his lips have left a mark. The sip goes flaming down my throat, and my belly shudders and shrinks, offended by what I've poured into it.

He chuckles. "You want more?"

I shrug okay.

"No you don't," he says sharply. "Remember that."

He tells me to turn on the radio. I lean over the stereo resting beside the television and nudge the tuner across fields of static. All I can find is classical, a whiny violin and no words to go with it. Sad as a book with no pictures.

My father sits up in his chair and puts the glass between his feet. "I used to play violin," he says. "Did you know that?"

"No."

"You didn't know that?" he says, as if I don't know how to spell my own name. "In the Gulf, I knew a girl who played the violin so beautifully she would make you cry."

My mother enters the room, her cheeks shiny with cold cream. On her way to the kitchen, she eyes me, my dad, his glass.

"She has school tomorrow," my mother says.

He nods emphatically. "Yeah, yeah, we're just talking."

"Don't talk too much." She clangs the plates around in the sink.

He glares at her back, but the venom soon drains from his face, leaving behind a colorless resignation. He turns to me and shrugs. "She hates me."

After my mother leaves, my father puts his elbows on his knees and leans forward, his eyes closed. I wonder if he is dozing off. The song on the radio softens and slows, at which point my father takes an imaginary violin in his left arm, pointing it downward, and tilts his chin against it. He draws his invisible bow along with the single, smooth note from the radio's violin, his face perfectly still, as if listening for his own pulse. The slipper with the exposed toe begins to tap against the orange carpet. The melody gathers force, and he dives into his performance, elbowing the air, rocking back and forth as he inscribes the space between us with song. The music climbs inside his body, takes possession of him like a long charge of electricity. Trills of joy, half and whole notes, reckless crescendos. I am lost in a rapture of admiration.

When he has drawn the last note, I clap until my father stands and takes a wobbly bow. He puts both hands on my head, which he kisses as if in blessing. "You are the only one who gets me," he says. "Now go to bed."

The next morning, I wake up early enough for my mother to rake a brush through my tangled hair and plait it into a French braid. I whimper only once at the pain and sit patiently until she snaps the tail into a hair bobble with purple beads. On the school bus, I keep fingering the taut spine of the braid and sniffing the tail, fragrant with pomade.

All this effort is meant for Wes Lipkin, a boy in my class who double-blinks between every sentence, as if something is permanently stuck in his eye. Every Tuesday and Thursday morning, Wes gets on the school bus with his lunch box in one hand and a violin-shaped briefcase in the other. He sits alone, toward the front of the bus, with his back to the revelry at the rear, where kids are shouting, kneeling on the seats, bracing themselves for the turns and hills leading to school.

Usually I sit somewhere in the middle rows, but today I take the seat next to Wes. I say hello, but he doesn't answer. Wes is bent over his notebook, drawing something on the back, a swollen face with huge, veiny eyes and a tiny line for a mouth. "Is that you?" I ask.

"No," he says wearily, as if we've been through this before.

There is a placid quality to Wes Lipkin, the sorrow of a martyred saint, and a dorkiness that seems almost willful. His lunch box sits between us, the last of its kind in our grade.

Laying the end of my braid over my shoulder, purple beads in view, I ask Wes if he likes playing the violin. He glances at me as if this is a trick question. I say that my dad plays, and he's very good. Wes erases something. I say that my dad had to leave his violin behind, in the Gulf, when he came to America.

"Then he's probably not that good," says Wes. "I'd never leave my violin just anywhere."

I ask him if I can borrow his violin, just for a day, so my dad can play like he used to.

Wes bores into me with his big, blinking eyes. Then he says no, and goes back to drawing.

He doesn't give a reason, just *no*, again and again. I begin to suspect that he enjoys saying no to me, that it feels like he's saying no to everyone who has ever said no to him. All I can do is face forward, stuck with a view of a peeling pleather seat.

It is six p.m., and I am finished with my math homework. Sometimes my mother devises extra homework for no other reason than to keep me away from the television, but now that my father is here, she makes no comment when I tug a chair up next to his, just behind his line of sight. My feet don't reach the coffee table, like his do.

We watch Lynne Russell on Headline News, sneezing every so often because my mother is frying chili-rubbed fish. I keep saying "Bless you" under my breath, until my father says, "*Bleshyew, bleshyew*—what does it mean?"

"Something about hell," I fumble, embarrassed by the sudden beam of his attention. "So you won't go to hell."

I am relieved when he grunts and turns back to sensible Lynne Russell and her smooth, sculpted cheekbones. I look at the hair on the back of my father's hand, a wild tuft above each knuckle, in the exact place where lately I have seen one or two hairs of my own. This is my dad, I think. Today I am going to call him Dad. After my mother goes to bed, I will show him what I obtained at great risk during recess, when I asked to use the bathroom and instead jimmied open Wes Lipkin's locker. His violin case fit neatly into my drawstring gym bag. At the end of the day, I was the first one on the bus.

The opportunity doesn't seem to present itself. My father appears more haggard than he did yesterday evening. His eyes are bloodshot. Every so often he takes small sips of orange juice from a big plastic cup. When I ask for a sip, he says no so quickly that tears spring to my eyes. "I'm sick," he adds, without looking at me.

During the weather report, my mother comes in holding the violin case in both hands. She demands to know where I got it.

I say that my friend Wes Lipkin let me borrow it.

"Then why did Mrs. Lipkin call just now and say you stole it?" she asks. For this, I have no answer. I assumed that Wes Lipkin would figure it out, but I never guessed that he would tattle. "Lying and stealing—this is what you learn at school?"

She takes two long strides and I brace for the blow, but my father's outstretched legs are blocking her path. He has been sitting between us, looking back and forth like a spectator at a tennis match. "You're her father," my mother reminds him. "Yell at her!"

My father sits up with the cup in his hand, spilling a bit of juice on his knee before setting it under the coffee table. He turns to me, dropping his voice low. "Why did you do it?" My face goes hot and cold at once. I pinch my own thigh. "Huh? Why did you steal that thing?"

"I wanted to hear you play."

My mother and father stare at me.

"So you can play like you did last night," I say, a strange sense of panic filling my chest. "The way you used to play over there, in Dubai."

My mother snorts. "Play what?"

My father listens to me, for the first time, without scorn, his face opening up with faint surprise. Then he glances up at my mother and waves me away. "What kind of nonsense. I don't know what she's saying."

"Remember, with the radio?" I mimic his playing, but he won't look at me anymore and my arms fall to my sides. I try to steady my voice. "Your friend, the girl who plays the violin?"

"Girl?" my mother says in a voice that is small and strained. It does sound strange when I say it aloud. His friend, a girl.

My mother turns to my father, and as his eyes search mine, I understand that he isn't lying. He simply doesn't remember. He doesn't remember saying, *You are the only one who gets me*, the loveliest compliment of all my eight years.

Quietly, my mother tells me to go to my room and get dressed. She says that she will drive me to the Lipkins' so I can apologize and return the violin.

Before I have closed the door to my room, the fight has begun. Their voices are subdued and tense, nearly unintelligible until they start shouting, and I learn certain truths at terrible speeds: there is a woman in the Gulf, a woman he left behind for my mother's visa, a woman who may be watching the road and waiting for him as we once did. And though none of us will ever again call up her presence, the woman will take up space in our house, as ubiquitous as a vapor, a woman at my window with one hand on the sill, tapping on the glass with the bow of her violin.

My mother and father stop fighting only when the old man who lives below us bangs his broom against his ceiling. The old man usually delivers this complaint when I'm jumping rope indoors, and for once I am grateful for his intervention. My parents fall silent.

I hear the door to my mother's bedroom slam shut. I am still sitting at the foot of my bed, gripping the bedpost, waiting to know what has changed and what will stay the same. Through the wall I hear the sound of soft, stifled weeping.

By the time I get up and pad quietly to my mother's door, the weeping has stopped. I know how to comfort her, how to crawl into her bed and hang my leg over her hip the way we used to sleep when it was just the two of us. I slip into her unlit room, and as my eyes adjust to the darkness, I make out a hunched shape—my father. Alone, he is sitting on the edge of the bed, his back to me. When he wipes the corner of each eye with the heel of his hand, he seems no older than I am, and I will remember this gesture for years. I linger in the still pool of his sorrow. Quietly as I can, I slip back into the hall and close the door.

The Scriptological Review:
A Last Letter from the Editor

...

This is not a guide to good handwriting. You'll find no dos and don'ts, no dotted lines here. If that's what you're looking for, try *Cursive First,* a workbook force-fed to me at the age of eight, when the nuns tried to mold my hand around the rubber pencil grip of conformity.

What you're reading is the final copy of *The Scriptological Review,* a journal dedicated to the social analysis of handwriting. Our inaugural issue appeared two years ago, with a cover story titled "Slanty Signatures and Secret Turmoil: The Correlation Between High Cursive Slant and Low Self-Esteem." In this, we analyzed a letter from John Wilkes Booth, whose cursive was brambled with signals that the lay reader would likely ignore, such as intraletter gaps and distended *a*'s and *o*'s.

If you're still reading, then it's likely that you are a subscriber and a scriptophile, but for the remaining fraction who have happened upon this issue on a bus seat or in a dentist's office (or propping open a window, as I found my mother's copy of Volume IV), let me introduce myself.

My name is Vijay Pachikara, and I am presently the editor of *The Scriptological Review*. My mom is listed on the masthead as "publisher-at-large," but all she provides is the funding and the office space. I set up shop in her basement a year ago, and the commute from my bedroom couldn't be better.

As long as my mom handles the funding, I don't mind if she wants to while away her time with her boyfriend, Kirk Bäumler. Kirk is reliable and handy, like a good garden tool, a man of patience and resolve who once felled a cedar tree on his property and fashioned it into a dugout canoe. There may be much to admire about men like Kirk, but his handwriting tells another story.

Exhibit A: *Inscription from Birthday Card to Vijay from Kirk*

Happy 22ⁿᵈ Vijay
I hope this year brings you joy!

Best
KIRK

Consider the narrowness of the *e*-loops, so sharp that they verge on lowercase *i*'s, a recurring sign of neediness. Also note the castrated *y*.

I tried to persuade my mom to note as much while she was packing for their overnight trip to Nashville, but she was too busy fitting her belongings into her suitcase, as pleased as if she were assembling the last pieces of a jigsaw puzzle. Kirk had urged her to come away with him to the Bahamas, but she refused to leave town for more than a night. I told Kirk that this was for the best, since I'd need her to make a few purchases from the photocopy store, where my credit card had been repeatedly declined. Kirk bit his lower lip, as he often does when I mention the *Review*.

Kirk has been sore ever since I wedged copies of the *Review* under the fenders of his employees' cars two weeks ago. Apparently, the boardroom drones of Steak Shack Inc. have no sense of imagination or innovation, save the daughter of one guy, who called the number on the back of the magazine and asked if she could "sign up for the writing club." Caitlin lived with her parents, said "um" a lot, and had less than a rudimentary comprehension of scriptology. Maybe she was bored. I was about to give her directions to my house when we were interrupted by what sounded like her father in the background: "Who're you talking to, Cait? It's been forty-five minutes."

I heard her say, "No one . . ." before she promptly hung up.

A few days later, Kirk and my mom returned from Nashville. For half an hour, we bleeped through their digital photos: jubilant smiles, sad khaki shorts, both of them flanking a painted guitar twice their height. Her, in a rare moment of unabashed laughter, her hand at her heart, a gaudy rock on her finger, a ring I didn't recognize. Him, standing beneath a sign that read GRAND OLE OPRY HOUSE, his arms spread wide as if waiting for a huge hug. (See Exhibit A, Neediness.)

"Well," I said finally. "Well, great. Now my news. Mom, I've been thinking about the next issue of the *Review*—" I looked at Kirk pointedly. "Kirk, could you . . ." I glanced at the door. Kirk. Door. He sat there like a dog that didn't know its own name.

He told me that he and my mom had gotten engaged.

"Yeah, I get it. I'm not surprised per se, if that's the response you're looking for. But congrats to you both." My mom and Kirk traded glances, communicating in the not-so-secret parlance of married people. "Can we move on?"

Kirk moved on to trashing the *Review*. He recommended that I shut down operations, because he and my mom would be married soon. My mom would be the wife of the CEO of Steak Shack Inc., and the CEO could not afford phone calls like the one he'd received yesterday evening from a board member who had threatened to "take action" if he caught me communicating with his twelve-year-old daughter again.

Accordingly, my mom would be withdrawing all money from my budget, thus halting operations.

I stared at her. Wincing, she rubbed her chest, where her skin had lightly burned. "Did you know she was twelve?" my mom asked.

"Obviously not, Mom."

"Why were you talking to her for forty-five minutes?"

"Because," I said, looking only at her, "she was listening."

This prompted a certain tone of voice my mom takes when she thinks I've lost the bread-crumb trail to normalcy. She asked if I needed to talk to Dr. Fountain, a heavily perfumed shrink I'd been seeing off and on throughout the year. It always made my face burn when she brought up Dr. Fountain in front of Kirk.

"As I was saying." Maybe I repeated that phrase a few times while flipping the pages of my notebook, in which my scrawl was deeply, deliberately engraved. "The next issue will be dedicated to Dad."

In our two years of circulation, *The Scriptological Review* has published a biannual personafile on historical or celebrity figures. Each signature, each strand of unraveled scripts, has led to analyses of the type rarely recorded in the humdrum biography or rise/fall/rehab biopic. Some highlights include Benjamin Franklin ("If Left Is Wrong, I Don't Want to Be Right"), the Marquis de Sade ("Outer Loops and Inner Demons"), and Martha Stewart ("White Space 101"). In light of such figures, one might question the relevance of a personafile concerning my father, Prateep.

But this personafile has been long in the making, a goal of mine ever since the inaugural issue of the *Review*. My mission is to enlarge what my dad was reduced to, the five lines of an obituary, because we are survived not by memories but by what we leave behind in print or picture, and how are five stunted lines to span the breadth of a man's life?

Take Exhibit B, a telling excerpt lifted from a letter sent by my father to my mother in the first two weeks of their marriage, after he had flown ahead of her to the United States. She would be following shortly, her first time leaving her family in Bangalore.

Exhibit B: *Excerpt from Letter Sent by Prateep J. Pachikara to His Wife, Annamma*

LOVE,
Prateep

The rest of the letter is in Malayalam, and thus illegible to me, but scattered here and there with English words like "Johnny Carson" and "Cheerios." These few words are pinholes of light in an otherwise impenetrable wall. I once asked my mom to translate the letter, and with a cursory glance, she returned it to me. "He says he has no friends except for Johnny Carson. He eats a lot of Cheerios. He hates his life." She refused to say more and told me to remove my boxers from the dryer.

The sample above speaks volumes. Note the incomplete *a* and *o*, how the two ends of a line yearn to meet. However despairing the words that precede it, the *a* and *o* reveal a man in search of something, or someone, a man who has not yet drained his deepest cisterns of hope.

I tried to appeal to my mom in private, the day after her return from Nashville, but she was standing over her bathroom sink, smearing a sliced grape all over her face. She'd read somewhere that grape acids would tighten her pores, and she wanted to look good for the wedding. She planned to grape her face every other day until the Big Day.

"That's a lot of grapes," I said, without waiting for her to tell me exactly how many. "Can we talk about the *Review*?"

"Come here, Viju." She flapped her hand at me. "Closer."

I thought she was going to hug me. Instead she swiped the grape across my forehead and laughed.

"Mom, I'm serious."

"Are you ever not serious?" she teased, and tossed the deflated grape into the trash. She exercised her facial muscles by widening her mouth, knitting and raising her eyebrows. Meanwhile, I explained a few of the diverging schools of thought I would explore in the personafile: Did the prongs of the double *e* indicate charges of excitement or alarm? Was *L* height and *y* length directly or inversely proportional to extrovert behavior? Was she actually siding with Kirk on this one?

"I am on both sides," she said, same as when Kirk and I feuded over the benefits of organic produce. Eventually she stopped buying the grocery strawberries we both once loved, the super-sweet diploid mutants, and started bringing back from the farmers' market a carton of sour red nubs. Then, as now, she repeated the same refrain: "Kirk is just thinking about our future." This time, she added: "He could find you a job, you know."

"I have jobs. I have lots of jobs." I was happily getting by on an assortment of pet-sitting and telemarketing gigs, reluctant to leash my days to a normal nine-to-five. I lived with my mom out of both financial necessity and professional convenience, since my dad's study was the base of my operations. I used the bottom drawer of his gray metal desk to archive all his handwriting samples, compiled from a multitude of sources—viz., old address books, tax returns, receipts, electric bills, grocery lists, aerogrammes, and a yellow Post-it on which he'd scribbled an unattributed quote: ". . . *by the Lord God of hosts, the Holy, who made you of the happy breed and me of the stricken, He alone knowing the aught of making mortal things, I am lonely!*" Everything in my project was filed chronologically; subfiled according to Professional, Personal, Financial, or Miscellany; and sub-subfiled according to recipient. And out of this would grow, piece by piece, a mosaic of my father.

"Wait," I said, alarmed. "What'll happen to the house?"

"We'll sell it. Kirk has more than enough room for the three of us in his place." What Kirk has is a white colonial propped up by Doric columns in which there are more bidets than books of substance. "We'll have the engagement party on the lawn."

"But the desk, you have to let me keep Dad's desk. I think, Mom—" Here I took her sticky hand. "I think Kirk might like the *Review* if he gave it a chance. If he really read it. Or if he took the time to listen to what I've noticed about his checkbook, because in all those signatures, his *B*'s are turning into lemniscates, which, according to the literature, suggest dizziness and lack of pause or breath."

My mom removed her hand from mine. "What were you doing with his checkbook?"

"I found it in his desk. Last time I was there." I hesitated. My mom's nostrils were flaring: a bad sign. "I needed to know something about him."

"Then just talk to him! Did you ever think of that?" She frowned at the counter and shook her head, as if refusing to envision what I'd done. "You should not go snooping around, Viju. Kirk will tell you what you want to know. He's very open. He doesn't just"—she searched for a word—"disappear for a whole day."

She was referring to my dad. True, he had had a tendency to seclude himself from time to time, though we always knew he was in the guest room. He would lock himself in and answer to no one, not when I crouched down to speak through the crack, not when my mom set a cup of chai by the threshold. The mug sat there, cooling. Sometimes I stood with my ear pressed to the door, but he always told me, coldly, to leave him alone. The next morning, I would find him brewing coffee or whistling at his desk. When asked what he had been doing in the guest room, he always gave the same perky excuse: "Just lying down."

A few months ago, my mom went snooping through my dad's study, alarmed by the number of hours I was spending down there. In my dad's desk, she discovered a mission statement—five pages, handwritten, erudite but sloppy in places—in which I detailed my earliest theories on *i* dots and *t* strokes. Somewhere in there, I may have mentioned the resemblance between my dad's writing and my own. I may have written along a margin: *Do certain types of t's, like certain disorders, run in the family?*

Soon after, my mom made my first appointment with Dr. Fountain. (Before her, it was Dr. Dan, and before him, Dr. Golden, whom I actually liked, in spite of the halitosis.) As far as my studies were concerned, Dr. Fountain showed a condescending interest. I could never read what was going on behind her eyes; they were the sharp, devoid blue of an antique doll.

She tried to diagnose me with trauma-related stress disorders. Unfortunately for Dr. Fountain, I didn't hear voices. I never considered cutting myself. I didn't wash my hands two hundred times per day with two hundred packaged bars of soap. Over and over, Dr. Fountain asked me about my dad, how I found him, what I saw, how I felt. I gave clear answers. When our time was up, she scribbled a prescription for a drug whose company rep had probably wined and dined and plied her with samples the week before. (I tried the little pills, oblong and caution-tape yellow, but they doused every bright idea I had. My brain went to putty, stretching in all different directions at once, slackening. I had deadlines to meet, articles to write. I went off the pills immediately.)

Dr. Fountain showed specific interest in the one item I offered her—a postcard of a koala bear wreathed in white fur, beside the words "G'day mate!" On the back, my dad had penned a note to my third-grade teacher, Sister Lorraine, which I've reproduced here.

Exhibit C: *Koala Postcard from Prateep J. Pachikara to Sister Lorraine*

Dear Sister Lorraine,

As requested, I am coming to school today to discuss my son Vijay.

Regards,
Prateep J. Pachikara

This is the last known record of his writing, dated March 3, a week before his death. Luckily, I saved the postcard in my binder's plastic sleeve, charmed by the koala but oblivious to the signals within the writing itself—viz., the clockwise curl at the beginning of my *V*, which unravels to a straight and sterile line in his notes to others, but here, so much emotion is clutched in that tiny rose before the plummeting fall, the confident pivot, and the upward rise and arch that hangs over the *i* like a protective branch.

Sister Lorraine had called the meeting because of my fresh interest in sorting through garbage. Cafeteria garbage, classroom garbage: nearly every wastebasket held my interest if Sister Lorraine had passed over it. From the bin beneath her desk, I recovered a comb with broken teeth, a return receipt for wool socks, a cup of wild blueberry yogurt scraped so clean she must have been starving. After I was caught poking through the trash in the faculty bathroom, Sister Lorraine found a litter museum in my locker.

When my dad came in for the meeting, he could see what drove my studies: Sister Lorraine. Pert, pretty, short-haired, slim-fingered, citrus-smelling Sister Lorraine. I don't recall her face so well anymore, but it's her aura I remember, a beatific glow for all those who earned her favor.

Which I had not. My dad listened to Sister Lorraine's concerns, stroking the ends of his mustache between thumb and forefinger, something I occasionally mimicked during class, though there was only a single tentative whisker on the corner of my lip. That day I kept my clammy hands in my lap.

My dad began to report to Sister Lorraine what he had read concerning the field of garbology, explaining that refuse analysis informed a range of fields, from marine biology to corporate espionage. "So the question, Sister, is not 'What kind of child is interested in trash?' but 'What does this child hope to find in the refuse?'"

The word "refuse" still murmurs in my mind, a delicate, scholarly term hovering just above my eight-year-old reach. My dad turned to me, as if it were my chance to reveal what I was looking for. I went warm with embarrassment.

Later, in the car, he confronted me with the obvious. "Nuns can't get married, you know."

"What about in *The Sound of Music*?" I said.

"She married Captain Von Trapp, not one of the Von Trapp children. That would be a very different movie."

I sank down, small in my seat.

We stalled at the railroad tracks, the signal blinking and clanging while the traffic arm lowered to block our path. "You are a strange bird," my father observed, studying me as if trying to put a name to my face. "I was, too."

I saw the similarity as a good thing, but my dad looked lost in murky thoughts. The signal flashed red in the corner of my eye; I could feel the roar of the oncoming train beneath my feet. He held me in his gaze and then, with a sigh, let go. "Come on, already," he groaned, just as the train whooshed by.

Those were the days leading up to his death, and in that time, my father drank no more than usual. He left us no note. That morning, as I hurried out to catch the school bus, I glanced at the closed door of the guest room, but how could I know then of the pills in his pocket, half in the bottle and half down his throat? How could I know he wouldn't wake up, dress, and step into the shoes he had left by the door, because in his pajamas and robe he was already gone?

·

At the engagement party, I was stuck at a table with Kirk's mother. She glowered at the surroundings—the tiki torches staked around the lawn, the paper lanterns strung along the wooden stairs that led down to an artificial lake, blurred by mist. She had me bring her a gin and tonic from the bar and kept chewing on the straw even when she wasn't sipping. "Why are you sweating so much?" she demanded of me. "And you keep looking around. Who are you looking for?"

"Kirk," I said.

"Oh." She rolled her eyes. "Good luck. He's probably chasing after your mother."

And Kirk was wisely avoiding his own. I resolved to corner him in an hour or so, when he'd be tipsy enough to feel magnanimous about my proposal. I kept my notecards in my pocket in case I were to lose my train of thought; between them I'd paper-clipped my dad's koala postcard, to use as a visual aid.

My mom had no idea about my plans. She was busy circulating between kitchen and party and wine cellar, steering children away from the tiki torches. At one point, as she was talking to someone, Kirk came up behind her and put a hand on her shoulder, and she rested her hand over his without turning around to see who it was. I don't know why, but that small gesture made me feel something other than hatred or envy—maybe warmth, and a little sadness.

I excused myself from Kirk's mother and descended the stairs to the lake. I stood at the end of the little pier where a paddleboat was bobbing on the water. Before me the lake seemed to widen in a gray-black haze, and all at once uncertainty swept over me, as it still does sometimes, because I seem to find comfort only in fragments, because there is something impossible about shoring them into something larger, just as there was something futile and frightening about the borderless world beyond that lake, how the sky exhaled and expanded with no outer limit, the stars slipping farther and farther away, like everyone I loved.

I took out the first notecard and mumbled my way through my introduction: *Kirk, I know we haven't gotten along in the past . . . come to an understanding . . . scriptology is central to my life . . . my father . . . a few samples from his persona-file . . . my father . . .*

"Vijay, time for cake cutting!"

I turned to find my mom easing her way down the last few steps in her heels. She stopped short of joining me on the pier and gave a winning smile, her teeth lacquered with wine. "What are you doing down here, Viju? Practicing your toast?"

"What toast? You didn't say I'd have to give a toast."

"You weren't going to say something?" She looked slightly crestfallen. I joined her on the bank. "Then what's that card you were reading?"

I tried to shrug my mom away, which only heightened her interest; she snatched the notecard from my hand. It seemed childish to grasp for it back so I stood there as she read it, watching her face cloud over.

"You won't understand without the visual aid," I said, pulling out the koala postcard and handing it to her.

She looked at the card in her left hand and the card in her right, as if they had materialized out of nowhere. "This is what you were planning to say?"

"Just to Kirk. It won't take long, I promise. I just wanted to show him this thing, see . . ." I pointed out the initial between *Prateep* and *Pachikara,* but as I tried to gather myself beneath my mom's simmering glare, all my thoughts split apart like kaleidoscopic shards and re-fused into bright new patterns: suddenly the *J* seemed a mysterious glyph of some kind, its two loops freighted with greater meaning. I remembered first learning of lemniscates from high school math; it struck me as miraculous and maddening at the time, the idea of an upper limit always approaching a number, nearing ever closer but never quite attaining it.

It was some time before I noticed that my mom was watching me, stricken. "You can't give me a day, Viju? Not one day?"

"Look at this one." I tapped on the koala postcard, still in her hand. "See how steeply slanted those letters are, which is directly proportional to low self-esteem . . ." She turned the postcard over in her hands, staring blankly at the koala, and walked past me, stopping at the end of the pier. "And if you'd read Volume VI, you'd know that the concave, counterclockwise outer loop indicates an urgent regret, plus the gap—the *chasm*, really—between the *P* and the *a*—"

She turned to me, and I stopped. I'd never seen her shoulders slump like that. Even after my dad's funeral, she'd held herself straight and worn her grief like a veil that merely dimmed her view of the world. "Viju, when did you stop taking the pills?"

This I didn't see coming, but I tried to sound casual. "Oh, the Anafranil? Long time ago."

"Why?"

"It really messed with my head."

"Your head is already a mess!" she cried. I must have looked scared for a second because she lowered her voice. "If you don't want the Anafranil, then we'll meet with Dr. Fountain and try some other medicine."

"Yeah, maybe."

"What maybe?"

"Those are my decisions, Mom. I'm a grown-up."

"Oh, so grown." She leveled me a sad-eyed smile, and it made me feel like a kid again, a boy who didn't realize how bad things really were. "I can't go ten feet without worrying where you are."

We stood there in silence, the water lapping all around

us, the paddleboat knocking against the post. I looked at my mom; her arms were folded. Panic caught me by the throat. "Where's the postcard?" I asked.

She said nothing.

I met her at the end of the pier, and she stepped aside, looking down at the water.

"Leave it," she said, taking urgent hold of my arm. "Come back with me."

She had tossed it into the water. My mom had tossed my world into the water. I felt a strange, slow lightening as my eyes scanned the surface, as I imagined its ink bleeding, its cursive unspooling to a line as flat as the distance from one person to another.

But as soon as I spotted the postcard drifting away, white side up, I plunged in after it as if by instinct (I'm not a swimmer), flailing and plowing until I felt it between my fingers. For we are bound, sometimes against our will.

I heard my mom yelling my name as I dog-paddled the few feet back to the pier. With one arm and both legs, I hugged the first slimy post I could grasp. She was kneeling above me, pulling on my shoulder as if she could hoist me out of the water, but I shook her away. She sat back on her heels, a rivulet of mascara down her cheek. "Give me the card, then," she said. "I won't throw it again, I promise."

She extended her hand, my mom, as she always has.

But I didn't give her the card, not immediately. I hung on to the post and listened to the faint murmur of the party in my waterlogged ears. Earlier in the evening, someone had asked her where she planned to honeymoon, and she had shrugged, saying, "Oh, not too far away." I thought of Kirk's Nashville photographs—the guitars, the tulips, the sights I had seen before—and all the far-flung journeys they could take instead if only they were free of me.

•

Since that day, I've secured an apartment and a full-time job at Red Carpet Cinemas, where for eight dollars an hour I stand behind a glass window and slide tickets through a cut-out hole, half price for seniors and children under twelve. Over time, I hope to acquire the funds to resuscitate the *Review,* but as bills accumulate (one of my roommates wants HBO on Demand), this hope grows ever distant.

Sometimes, on my lunch break, my mom visits. She and Kirk have been traveling again, and most recently they returned from the Bahamas with three straw hats. I hung mine on a nail in my room.

My mom looks good in her hat, her skin tan and varnished from the sun. She keeps asking if she can see my new place, but I keep telling her that I still have to put my room together, even though it was put together the day I moved in, with just space enough for a narrow bed and my father's desk.

My mom is given to worrying about me, but she's happy all the same. She's in love. I can tell because of the bill she signed at lunch the other day. *Anna Bäumler,* the umlaut not unlike a colon my dad once placed after my name on a birthday card with Superman on the cover, flying through the air beneath the words HAVE A SUPER-HAPPY BIRTHDAY!

Exhibit D: *Birthday Card from Prateep Pachikara*

Some might mistake the colon as a formal mode of address, used for letters of application or complaint. But note how this colon was made by a double stroke rather than a double stab. I have scanned and magnified each dot fourfold, revealing the slight eyelash left by the lingering pen. A double stroke, a double blink, a fond quickening of the heart.

Aerogrammes

. . .

In his first week at Renaissance Gardens, Mr. Panicker divided all the nurses into the black ones, the white ones, and the man-nurse, but never called any of them by name. Knowing names, it seemed, would root him there indefinitely.

His cousin Preeti had campaigned loudly against the move. "Our people don't use these kennels," she informed his son.

"Whose people?" Sunit said, scowling into the rusty insides of Mr. Panicker's toaster oven. Sunit and Preeti had flown in to help pack up the house and organize a yard sale. Mr. Panicker was sitting at the table, watching them, his knee still too weak to help.

"You don't understand," Preeti said. "You were raised here."

"And *you* didn't find Dad blacked out at the bottom of the stairs."

"We're only trying it out," said Mr. Panicker. He fingered the border of a CorningWare dish, the first plate he ever bought in this country, ugly and indestructible. "I might join Sunit in New York. We'll see."

"You hear things about these places," Preeti said. "Nasty things. People messing with people. People shooting people. You don't know." She pressed her lips together to demonstrate that she knew a great deal.

Though Mr. Panicker had yet to witness a shooting at Renaissance Gardens, Preeti's mantra had taken on a foreboding truth. The enrichment activities held little resemblance to the descriptions touted in the brochure, next to photographs of gently amused residents. The *pranayam* breathing sent him into a dizzy panic, while all around him residents huffed like angered bulls. He avoided Wii Wednesdays in the rec room, where people stared slack-jawed at the television, lurching around like marionettes. His rock garden resembled a pyre of turds.

Most of the time, Mr. Panicker watched *Perry Mason* marathons in his room. When he was not watching *Perry,* he was leaving message after message in Sunit's voice-mail box, addressing the deficiencies all around him, such as the dimensions of his room, which was so narrow that if he sat in his armchair and crossed one leg over the other, his foot hit the baseboard of his bed. "How am I supposed to cross my leg? I talked to the nurse about moving to a different room, but she says they are full." At the end of the week, Sunit's voice-mail box announced that it, too, was full.

There was one complaint Mr. Panicker couldn't imagine conveying to his son. The female neighbor to his right was carrying on with the male neighbor on his left.

It was a nocturnal affair. On certain nights, Mr. Panicker would hear the careful click of her door lock, followed moments later by the click of his. For the next thirty minutes,

Mr. Panicker had no choice but to stare at the light fixture overhead while the flex and squeak of bedsprings intruded through the wall. The woman was quiet, but toward the end, the man issued a morbid groan.

During the daytime, Mr. Panicker made sure to rush as much as his knee would allow past his neighbors' rooms. He wanted no leery, yellow smiles attached to such sounds, no details bolting him to this place at all. Some faces he could not ignore, like that of the receptionist who lifted her stenciled eyebrows whenever Mr. Panicker approached, knowing full well that his only inquiry, his constant inquiry, was whether Sunit had called.

In the second week, Mr. Panicker looked out his window to find an ambulance parked outside the front entrance. A gurney carrying a sheeted body waited behind it. Mr. Panicker went out into the hall and found the door to his neighbor's studio propped wide open. People were passing slowly by, peering into the empty room, where not a square foot of space remained on the walls, thick with framed photos, Hoosier pennants, a giant periodic table—so many places for the eye to dwell that the man might have succeeded in forgetting where he really was. Beneath the bed were a pair of red velvet booties, toes pigeoned inward.

Struck by a sudden sense of trespass, Mr. Panicker hurried down the hall, to the dining room.

Pink bunting festooned the walls in honor of Family Day, which Sunit had already called to say he could not attend. He had appointments in New York, with several production companies who were considering his script. Sunit rarely managed to send his father an e-mail, but he had sent a copy of his screenplay. It belonged to a growing subgenre, he said, not quite Bollywood, not quite Hollywood: Indians in America or England Torn Between Identities.

What most confused Mr. Panicker was how a thirty-eight-year-old man could still be writing about his twenty-year-old self, and how this thirty-eight-year-old man had not solved some of these issues by now, or at least shoved them aside to make new issues for himself, like how to stay with a woman for more than a year. Or how to find a job that offered a yearly vacation, not a year-long vacation interrupted by sporadic jobs.

Mr. Panicker peeled two hard-boiled eggs in solitude. His iron tablets left the taste of pennies in his mouth, and after only a bite of beloved pineapple, he had to lay down his fork and nudge the bowl away.

He tried to remember his dead neighbor's name. Bill? Hal? He could barely recall a face, only parchment wrinkles, liver spots, broken capillaries on the tip of a bulbous nose, the sorts of traits that made a brotherhood of every man here. If, by chance, the ambulance were to come for Mr. Panicker, would anyone in Renaissance Gardens recall his face, or even linger in his doorway?

On his way back to his own room, the door to the dead man's room was shut. As Mr. Panicker searched his pocket for his key, a woman walked down the hall and stopped before the door next to his. The door that belonged to the dead neighbor's mistress.

He snuck a glance at her. She wore a sweater hectic with flowers, a white turtleneck beneath it. Her hair was a long, limp curtain of silvery gray, nothing like the teased halos of most women her age. She looked over at him with moist, melancholy eyes that betrayed her nightly relations with the deceased. Mr. Panicker knew, and she knew that he knew.

He turned to her. The proximity of death made him bold.

"I am sorry for your loss," he said, the longest sentence he had spoken to another resident.

She blinked at him. "I think you mean Lily."

"Sorry?"

She aimed her chin at the door across the hall from his. "Him and Lily were the ones who went at it every night. Well. Except for last night." She gave him the patient smile of a pre-school teacher, but the words coming out of her mouth made his face go warm. "I'm May. Who are you?"

"My name is Hari Panicker."

"Panicker?" She grasped a piece of hair and wound it around her finger, like a little girl. "As in Panicker's Produce? On Chenoweth Lane?"

Hari smiled shyly, nodded. He had sold the store to a grocery chain that had renamed the place, somewhat hyperbolically in his opinion, Garden of Eden.

"I lived right around the corner!" May said. "I remember your commercial. The one with the talking ear of corn?" She cupped a hand to her ear. "Who listens to customers?"

"He was a paid actor. My cousin. But I paid him."

"What kind of name is Panicker? Are you Indian?"

"Yes."

Her hands shimmied in the air, a reaction he had never before received. "I wasn't sure because your skin is so pale. You could pass for Arab or Italian or Syrian or Egyptian . . ." Listing other pale-skinned nationalities, she unlocked her door. "Do you have a minute? I have a question for you."

He followed her into her studio. On one yellow wall hung a trio of gold frames, a fruit floating in each: apple, orange, and pear. Someone else must have hung the frames; they were too high for her to reach. Beneath these was a small breakfast table, tiled in cobalt blue, and a rocking chair in the corner with a quilt thrown over the back. She gestured to the rocking chair; he settled carefully into it.

"You have family coming today?" Mr. Panicker asked.

"No, no kids for me." May opened the top drawer of her dresser and pushed some items aside until she surfaced with an open aerogramme. "Hah! Here it is." She offered it to him with both hands.

Mr. Panicker had always loved the slick texture of an aerogramme between his fingers. He remembered plucking them from his old mailbox, squinting and turning each one around and around like a kaleidoscope, as there were always more messages that his mother had crammed up and across the margins. In this one, the print was large and earnestly etched, wasting vast margins of blue on every side.

"Is this a girl or a boy?" she asked. "The name at the bottom."

Dear Miss May Daly,

Hello, my name is Satyanand Satyanarayana. I am ten years old. I live in Bombay India. I like to swim and play cricket. I also like to draw pictures of tigers and elephants. But I do not have a lot of time to swim or draw because I have to beg for food so my mother and I can eat.

Miss Daly, when you were waking up in your bed this morning, Satyanand was waking up on a bed of wet newspapers. When you were taking a shower, Satyanand was bathing in waters where children were defecating a few yards upstream. With your donation, little Satyanand can buy resources, medicines, and food for the month. Thank you for your sponsorship and continue to keep Satyanand in your heart.

"Boy," he said.

"Are you sure? Because he's my Street Angel now, and they

said they'd send a picture but they didn't and it'd be nice to be sure."

"Definitely boy."

She brought the aerogramme close to her face, as if its nearness could prove him right. "You can adopt a Street Angel from just about any third world country, you know. I requested India." She took a step toward him. He leaned back in the rocking chair, cornered by her curiosity. "What's Bombay like?"

"Bombay? Dirty."

"Dirty? That's all?"

He'd never been outside the airport in Bombay, only remembered his plane touching down, the tarp and tin sheeting of slums reeling like a filmstrip past his window. "Bombay, I don't know very much. I am from Kerala, much south of there. It's a beautiful place. Coconut trees, paddy fields. God's own country, they call it." She still looked vaguely disappointed. He felt like a travel agent, unable to sustain her interest.

"Is it close to Bombay?"

He told her to hold on a moment, springing up from the rocking chair so quickly that he had to steady himself on the armrests.

Minutes later, he returned with a map, which he unfolded on her bed. He pointed out the sliver of land called Kerala, barely the size of a nail clipping. They spoke Malayalam, he said, like him. Cricket was a more sophisticated form of baseball, with slimmer players in prim sweater vests. In Bombay, the boy most likely swam in the sea, not a swimming pool.

"But isn't the water polluted?" she asked.

He rolled up the map like a sacred scroll. "Our people have excellent immune systems."

•

May began a habit of stopping by Mr. Panicker's room before every meal and accompanying him to the cafeteria, where they sat with people she knew. Mr. Panicker tried to engage in small talk, though his attention often swayed to the window, where mango-colored leaves were beginning to shiver against their branches. Mealtime provided him with some daily distraction, but still there was the grit he could not ignore, the dusty blinds like lengths of bone-gray ribs, the potent smell of detergent in the pillowcases.

Before his mind could wander too far, May would guide him back into the conversation with a question. He was grateful to her because he had never excelled at making his presence known among groups of people. Sometimes the accumulation of his silence seemed to heap upon him, as slowly as snow, until he felt he could no longer be seen.

Mr. Panicker was far more at ease when they were alone. She had consulted him for her response to the first aerogramme, and on his recommendation, she had asked Satyanand what he thought of the cricket star Sachin Tendulkar. When Satyanand's second aerogramme arrived, she brought it directly to Mr. Panicker.

Dear Miss Daly,

Thank you so much for your twenty dollar donation. With this money, I was able to buy chappals for school and plenty of rice for my family to last the month.

"What's a *chappal*?" May asked.
"A kind of sandal. Or flip-flops."

In response to your question, though I like to play cricket, I am not familiar with players as I do not have a television or a radio.

"Maybe you should stop this Street Angel business," said Mr. Panicker. "It could be a trick."

She held the letter to her chest. "Where did you get that idea?"

"What kind of Indian boy doesn't know Tendulkar?"

Her eyes flitted over the letter with affection. "My boy."

Watching her, Mr. Panicker remained silent. It didn't seem so wrong at the time, the way her fingers were breezing back and forth across the writing. She deserved that moment of peace, and he wanted to preserve it for her, if he could, in return for all the small ways she had thus far preserved him.

By the end of the month, Sunit began calling Mr. Panicker again, bearing better, if not good, news. Mr. Panicker could hear the fraying hope in Sunit's voice as he explained how his manager was passing the script to someone else and then someone else; it was widely described as "hot."

"Sounds like a game of Hot Potato," said Mr. Panicker.

Sunit paused, then forced a chuckle. "Yeah, it's good to keep a sense of humor about these things in case, well . . ." He paused. "So anyway, if you really can't handle it at Renaissance Gardens, then we'll move you up to New York, I guess. Once I get this thing sold."

"But don't sign a lease or anything, not until I get there. It should be a place big enough for both of us. I have my savings, so we can manage it."

"We, like you and me? Roommates?"

"Who else would I mean?"

"I was thinking of two separate apartments. Maybe in the same neighborhood or something. I need some space, Dad."

"Space is overrated in this country."

"We'll see, okay? Let's just cross that bridge later."

"Oh, whatever," Mr. Panicker said, angry that he could not say what plagued him: that he would die soon. This he knew, just as he'd known it at the top of the basement stairs with that one light-headed step, the ground he had walked for seventy-six years disappearing from under his feet.

May read aloud the next two aerogrammes as Mr. Panicker sat in the rocking chair, poised like a director with his hands in steepled prayer, his ankle perched on his knee. Each letter contained a troubling inconsistency. Satyanand Satyanarayana had no opinions on Bollywood stars; twice he referred to Shah Rukh Khan as a "she."

Despite his doubts, Mr. Panicker delighted in elaborating upon every letter May received. He described Satyanand's possible route to school, how he and his friends would have to wend through the crush of taxis and rickshaws and fling themselves onto the train—the older boys hanging out the doorway if they were so bold—and how the rushing wind would dry his washed hair cold and crisp.

He spoke of his own son only when she asked him how Sunit was doing. "Sunit is Sunit," Mr. Panicker said, before changing the subject. Eventually she learned to stop asking.

He would have been happy to limit his social circle to her alone, but May begged him to attend the Fall Sock Hop. It was held in the dreaded rec room, site of Wii Wednesdays and Film Noir Fridays, by a troop of local Boy Scouts. A news crew arrived to tape the event; one lady told the camera, "It's just so lovely to have young people with us. The girls never have enough partners to go around."

Mr. Panicker hid behind the punch bowl until May hooked

her arm through his and steered him onto the floor. The Boy Scouts held their ladies at arm's length, shifting their gazes around the room, avoiding one another's eyes. None of the ladies seemed to care. They rocked and swayed to the crooning music, chins raised, eyes cloudy with pleasure and memory.

Mr. Panicker held May's hands in front of him, as if gripping the reins of a horse. Instead of risking any leg movement, he stayed in place, bending his knees according to his own erratic rhythm. Eventually he was lulled by the scent of baby powder on her skin, the rise and fall of the music. He twirled her under his arm. Later, May got him to admit that he was enjoying himself, even if he had abstained from the conga line.

A breeze swept through Mr. Panicker's lungs while he walked around the courtyard. It was early in the day, the clouds pink-bellied and young; dry leaves swirled in midair like shoaling fish. Today was Mercy's birthday.

His wife had never wanted any fuss made on her behalf. Mercy was tidy, brisk, uncomplaining, always the first to finish her meal before urging Sunit to eat up, eat fast, as if talking were a waste of time. She rarely disclosed her own preferences to Mr. Panicker, whether they were discussing a school for Sunit or a television program to watch. She always deferred to Mr. Panicker with "Whatever you like." After a while, he stopped asking her opinion.

Once, for her birthday, he surprised her with a gift delivered to their home: a double-mattressed DreamSupreme, as wide as twice his wingspan, with pillows fat and sugar white. It filled their bedroom, and for once, Mercy smiled and said, yes, she liked it. For two more years, he and his wife slept soundly, a whole wingspan of space between them, until she fled the

DreamSupreme for Sunit's math teacher, and whatever banana peel of a cot a math teacher might have to offer.

Sunit was only seven when they moved to America. Back then, Mr. Panicker told the boy to sleep in his own bed, and though the darkness seemed smothering, the hallways choked with shadow, Sunit agreed to sleep alone. But on some mornings, fresh from another drowning dream, Mr. Panicker would roll over to see his son, a snoring resolute curl on the other side of the bed. Always Sunit avoided his father on those days, ashamed perhaps, though Mr. Panicker never mentioned it. Nor did he mention how every morning was a trial, and sometimes it was simply the weight of Sunit's presence that gave Mr. Panicker the strength to rise.

When Mr. Panicker returned to his room, he found a pink slip on his door with the heading WHILE YOU WERE OUT. Sunit's name was scribbled below this, and a check mark was leaping out of the small box next to URGENT.

Mr. Panicker dialed the numbers, gripped the phone with both hands.

"Dad?" Sunit answered.

"What happened? Tell me."

"No, it's good news—I got an offer! I got an offer from Two Tigers, the company I was telling you about, the guys who produced the road-trip movie with the lesbian and the arranged marriage? The woman who played the lesbian read it and she wants to costar."

"Is there a lesbian in your story?"

"What? No. I just got the call from my manager, so I don't know much yet, but I think like thirty thousand. It's called an option. I'm *optioning* my script."

"Now what? What does this mean?"

"It means," Sunit said, with the enthusiasm of a game-show host, "you should come to New York!"

Mr. Panicker was sure that Sunit had no idea when or how this grand prize would be awarded.

"I already spoke to Preeti Auntie," Sunit said. "She wants you to come live with her in Queens."

"You called Preeti?"

"Yeah, we've been talking for a few days," Sunit said. "I told her we'd hire someone to stop by every day, and she said she'd love for you to have the room next to Biju and Binoy."

Mr. Panicker cringed at the memory of the greasy doorknobs in Preeti's house, Biju and Binoy's hair gel traveling from their spiny coifs to their hands, to the doorknobs, to Mr. Panicker's hands and wherever else.

"But how close are you to Queens?" Mr. Panicker asked.

"Like forty-five minutes."

"You'll visit?"

"Of course, Dad. When I have the time."

"I can't talk to those boys. They have no sense."

"Dad, I'm at Preeti Auntie's place right now."

Preeti picked up another phone in the house. "What is there to argue? You'll live next to Biju-Binoy."

"Aha, Preeti! I just mean I don't want to disturb you."

"Disturb, what disturb?" she said. "It disturbs me to care for family?" He pictured her with her telephone jammed under her chin as she arranged the items in her refrigerator just so, according to a system Mr. Panicker did not care to learn. "You're starting to talk like the *velumbin* you live with."

Mr. Panicker knocked on May's door for breakfast only to find that she had a visitor, a plain young woman sitting at the foot of the bed. She wore blue hospital scrubs, her hair knotted at the base of her neck. She was slicing an apple in her palm, a napkin spread across her knee.

Mr. Panicker offered to leave, but May, who had answered the door, waved him into the room. "See, look, Hari, this nice girl from church brought tea."

"Hi, I'm Leanne," the woman said, waving hello with her paring knife.

"Leanne," May agreed, nodding. "Sit, Hari, sit."

Mr. Panicker lowered himself into the rocking chair but declined when Leanne offered him his pick from a box of Constant Comment teas. He considered tea bags and tea to be two different things.

"At least have a muffin," Leanne said, nodding at the white paper bag on the blue tiled table. For a stranger from church, she seemed oddly at home in her surroundings, one leg folded beneath her on the bed. She would have been pretty, perhaps, if not for the downturned slant of her lips.

"You and May belong to the same church?" Mr. Panicker asked.

"Um . . . ," Leanne said, arranging the apple slices on a plastic plate. She glanced at May, who was rummaging through her dresser drawer, then shrugged. "I was baptized at her church. Haven't been since."

Mr. Panicker hesitated, confused, before May cut in: "I was just telling her about Satyanand." May pulled out a small packet of aerogrammes, secured with a rubber band, and happily fanned them at Leanne as if they were a stack of bills. "See? Look how many."

"I know," Leanne said, a humoring lilt to her voice. "You told me."

"I can't wait to show him," May said.

"Show me what?" Mr. Panicker asked.

"Not you. My son."

"I thought you have no children." Mr. Panicker sat forward, trying to understand. He looked at Leanne, who was also staring at May, though with less bewilderment, as if waiting for her to complete her sentence. May, meanwhile, was carefully depositing the stack of aerogrammes into her dresser drawer. "Who is this son?"

"Satyanand Satyanarayana." May uttered his name with nearly perfect pronunciation. She pushed the drawer shut and straightened the lacy runner draped across the top. "He's coming to visit. All the way from Bombay."

May went on about Satyanand with a distant, feverish look in her eye, mulling over what the boy might like to eat or see or do once he got here. Leanne listened placidly. Time and again, Mr. Panicker asked where May had gotten this idea, but she brushed off all his questions, concerned only with her own. "Do you think he's vegetarian?" she asked him, at which point Mr. Panicker stood up, flustered and queasy, and excused himself from the room. He had lost his appetite.

Ten minutes later, Leanne knocked on his door. "I'm sorry to bother you, Mr. Panicker, but would you mind walking me to my car?"

Only once they stepped outside did Leanne explain that she was May's grandniece. She worked at Baptist East as a nurse. He noted her height, a few inches taller than him, and wondered if this was the woman who had hung the framed fruit on May's wall.

Leanne didn't seem bothered by the news of May's "son." The year before, May had suffered a stroke, and ever since then, the delusions came and went. "A few months ago, she thought her bedroom was her office. She wouldn't see me unless I called and made an appointment. She got mad if I wore jeans."

"Maybe she has had another stroke," Mr. Panicker said. "Maybe that is why she's talking like this."

Leanne shook her head. "I had her squeeze my fingers. Her grip was fine, so that's a good sign."

"Good," he repeated. He watched his reflection in the window of her car, nodding.

"Good as it gets." Leanne smiled at him, heavily.

"Here, let me give you my info," she said, and began digging through her purse for a pen and paper. "I'd really appreciate it if you could keep an eye on her. Just let me know if she's acting funny? Or funnier than usual, I guess."

"I will not be here very much longer," he said. "This was to be a temporary stay for me."

"Oh." Leanne looked up. "Oh, good for you."

"But write it anyway. In case."

After she handed the paper over, Mr. Panicker brought it close to his face, making sure he could read all the numbers before he bid her good-bye.

All day long, Mr. Panicker avoided May's room. After lunch, he began to pack. He balled his socks and ordered them along the northern border of his suitcase, black, gray, black, blue, a mindless industry that freed him from his present and released him to his fruit-market days, arranging and rearranging boxes of fruit. They could have been clementines, these socks, if he ignored the rip of static between them, if he closed his eyes and thought himself back to the pine-green awning of Panicker's Produce on Chenoweth Lane, balancing tangelo against grapefruit, building pyramids and ziggurats as artful as the fruit market displays he'd known as a boy.

For years, Sunit had helped out at the store, until he entered high school and began losing all patience with customers. Once, when Mr. Panicker was ringing up a customer, Sunit beside him, clicking the price gun over a crate of bagged snacks, the customer looked at Sunit when asking for directions to the interstate. "Ask him," Sunit said, tilting his head at Mr. Panicker between clicks. "He knows English."

"No, the customer *isn't* king," Sunit said later, when Mr. Panicker scolded him. Mr. Panicker didn't know when that note of condescension had entered his son's voice, but after he left for college, it only hardened. If Mr. Panicker shared his opinion on Sunit's choice of studies, Sunit returned with terms like "entrenched" and "model minority," talking about Mr. Panicker's brain as if it were a tangle of ill-connected wires that only he could unravel.

Even now, Sunit thought he understood everything of Mr. Panicker's life, though he knew nothing of sitting in the fading light of a foreign room, running a finger over a tiny hole in the wall where someone must have tacked up a photo of loved ones, someone who was here at one time, and now was not. His son was ignorant of that hollow feeling. Mr. Panicker hoped he would remain so forever.

Before dinner, Mr. Panicker made himself knock on May's door, to see if she wanted to join him. There he would tell her that he would soon be leaving.

She had left her door slightly ajar. He nudged it open to find her hunched in her chair, frantic and flipping the petal-thin pages of her Bible. In her lap lay a pile of newspaper clippings, cards, pictures of saints, and all matter of memorabilia valuable only to her. She rubbed her hands together, her eyes flying about the room until her gaze landed on him.

"I lost them," she said. "I lost his letters."

"Whose?"

"What kind of a . . ." She clapped her hands to her mouth and began to whimper. "What kind of mother am I?"

"Did you look in your dresser?" Mr. Panicker asked.

"You look. Maybe I missed them." She hurried to her closet, but he hesitated. "Well, look, goddammit!"

He opened the drawer to a weedy tangle of graying brassieres and poked through them halfheartedly. She pulled an empty hat box from a shelf and dropped it behind her, then disappeared farther into the closet, her head bobbing among sweaters, a beaded blouse he had never seen her wear.

"Did you find it?" he asked.

She emerged empty-handed, murmuring a breathless prayer not unlike a nursery rhyme. She continued chanting while she turned her Bible upside down and shook it as violently as she could, though only a holiday card fell to the floor. "Saint Anthony, Saint Anthony, please look around, my son has been lost and cannot be found—"

Mr. Panicker tried to gently pry the Bible from her fingers, but she yanked it back with a force he hadn't expected.

"What do you know about it?" she said, the Bible splayed against her chest. "You don't know a thing!"

"I do know. I have a son."

"Son." She snorted. "No one's ever seen him around here."

He stared at her.

Gradually, her eyes softened and grew full. She sat down in her chair and searched the ceiling and walls, the windowsill, the paintings of bright, blank fruit.

"Stay here," he said. "I will show you."

•

Back in his room, Mr. Panicker rummaged through one of his suitcases, thumbed through papers, tossed books aside, rifled through shirts and pants. He found it in his dresser drawer, tucked inside a black address book: the photograph of Sunit in his school uniform—white dress shirt, navy shorts, backpack, *chappals*. His oil-slick hair had been combed into two distinct sections, one smaller than the other, a style that emphasized the gravity in his coal-black eyes. This, Mr. Panicker would tell her, was a real son, not a boy who existed only in letters.

And yet, her words, almost an accusation: *No one's ever seen him.*

He flipped farther through his address book in search of an adult picture of Sunit, but he discovered only more baby pictures. He had brought no pictures of Sunit as a man.

In the second drawer, beneath his sweaters, Mr. Panicker found a thick block of paper, secured with three shiny gold tacks. It was Sunit's ninety-page script, which he had said was "totally not autobiographical," though the cover page read, "An Indian-American man struggles against his overbearing single father." Here the script had remained for weeks, buried and unread. Mr. Panicker pulled the sweaters back over it.

He returned with the photograph and found May still seated, now wearing her glasses, staring at a fixed point out the window. He hovered in the doorway for a moment, unsure of himself. Their fight seemed far from her mind.

"See this," he said, and extended to her the photograph. She pulled her gaze from the window and looked down at his hand. He raised the photograph to her face, which remained blank, until she surprised him with a tiny, breathless cry.

"Satyanand," she breathed, and took the picture with both hands.

"Sunit," he corrected her.

"Satyanand," she said in the same drifting voice. "He looks sad."

Staring at the photo, Mr. Panicker remembered that he was the one responsible for his son's hairstyle. Usually, his wife combed Sunit's hair, but she had left them a few days before. Mr. Panicker recalled crouching over Sunit, moving the comb all too gently across his scalp. "Is this the right way?" Mr. Panicker had asked. In response, Sunit had looked in the mirror with the same expression he gave in the photo: neither approving nor disapproving but detached, set adrift.

After a time, Mr. Panicker said, "Sunit hated having his picture taken. He could never stay still."

"Satyanand," she corrected him, with the insistence of a child.

He looked more closely at the photograph and tried to remember that day, those days, the sense of coming ruin. In the months prior, Mercy had suffered from an edgy restlessness, one eye always on the window. Like mother, like son. Sunit would never visit him in Queens, and Mr. Panicker could not bear another slow abandonment.

"Satyanand Satyanarayana," May said to him, slowly, teaching him how to form the words.

Mr. Panicker nodded, repeating after her. "Satyanand."

She smiled, enchanted by the name settling like dust over the picture, and touched her forefinger to the boy's face, drawing from this some strength. They spent minutes like this without a word, and for Mr. Panicker, for now, this was enough.

Ethnic Ken

· · ·

My grandfather believed that the guest bathroom drain was a portal for time travel. I didn't mind his beliefs until they intruded on my social life, what little I had. My friend Newt and I were playing slapball against the side of my house—I was up to a record sixty-seven slaps—when my grandfather came outside and yelled at me in Malayalam for leaving a clot of my long hair in the bathtub drain, thereby blocking his route. His *mundu* was tied up like a miniskirt, wet scribbles of hair against his spindly calves. After calling me a "twit," my grandfather stormed back inside, leaving Newt to stare at me with a dispiriting combination of pity and shock.

"Did he call you a tit?" Newt asked.

"A twit. He's my grandfather," I added, as if that would explain things.

"He kinda seems like a jerk."

My grandfather wore house slippers with pom-poms at the toes. He could slice and deseed an apple in the palm of his hand. He believed that he was trapped somewhere in 1929, with the nine-year-old version of his wife, Ammu. He believed, without a doubt, that I was Ammu.

I could explain to Newt the firm but illogical architecture of my grandfather's delusions or I could stop inviting him to my house. So that was it for Newt and me.

In his absence, I played Barbie by myself, which wasn't as much fun without Newt and his Peaches n' Cream Barbie or Winter Wonderland Barbie, both of which he had borrowed from his older sister. My Barbie wore a gingham skirt and a saggy swimsuit that kept slipping down her chest in the middle of a conversation. My mom reminded me, often, that I was getting too old to play with dolls, being two months away from ten, but Newt was ten and he disagreed. He had even offered to steal one from his sister for me, a Ken. That was before he called my grandfather a jerk.

My mom would never buy me a Ken. I didn't even ask; it would've been too embarrassing to confess that I wanted my dolls to get romantic when I myself wasn't supposed to get romantic for another fifteen years. All I had left was a mannish knockoff of Barbie named Madge. Madge had big, flat feet and a chest like an afterthought, small and undefined. I chopped off her hair and knocked their heads together, but there were certain leaps that even my imagination just refused to make.

Two days after he chewed me out, my grandfather tried to make peace. We'd been through this before. I would be sitting in my room, racing through my homework to watch the TV shows everyone at school would be quoting the next day. My grandfather would wander in without a greeting, surveying my walls—the church calendar my mom had taped up, the poster of Jordan dunking with his tongue out. My grandfather had a quiet way of moving from room to room of our house, his hands behind his back, like a tourist observing the natives from a clinical distance.

This time, though, I was more than usually peeved and didn't look up from my vocab list when he stood beside me. He was wearing a fresh *mundu,* which now fell to his ankles, and over this, my mother's satin lavender robe, because satin, he said, made him feel expensive.

"Ammu," he said, "I cleaned the drain."

"Good."

"It's still not working." Sighing heavily, he seated himself on the edge of my desk, his lavender rump on the corner of my vocab sheet. "I didn't mean to yell at you, but my knees get tired, squatting in that tub."

He looked over his shoulder at me, and I nodded. Malayalam didn't come easily to me, but it was all he knew. By the time I'd piece together a complex sentence, he'd be rambling on to his next.

"What happened to your friend?" my grandfather asked. "The little one. He never comes around anymore."

"He moved."

"For good?" My grandfather perked up at the thought. He'd always been a little jealous of Newt and all the time I spent with him. "*Sarilla,* Ammu. We'll play our own games. We can play marbles—you love marbles."

He reminded me of the glass marbles I used to play with as a little girl, how I had my very own pouch of them in swirled reds and cloudy blues, how I used to play with my boy cousins by the tamarind tree. My grandfather got up and peered out the window by my desk. "Where is that tree . . ."

"I don't want to play marbles."

He seemed surprised, and slightly hurt. "Then what do you want to play?" He followed my gaze to the Barbie and Madge dolls, which were sitting upright on the corner of my desk. He took crew-cut Madge by the ankles and gave me a sidelong look. "Dolls? Still?"

"I have to do my homework."

I covered up the definitions column and tried to remember the difference between *imply* and *infer*. I did a few more words before realizing that my grandfather was still standing there, looking deep into Madge's tiny eyes. I could see his mind sliding in a wayward direction, as often happened at dusk. Something about the end of each day rattled him, made him jostle his dentures around for relief.

"Hey," I said gently.

He returned Madge to my desk and started cracking his knuckles, another tic. "But the tree . . . where is it?"

Here is where my mom would have insisted that there was no tamarind tree, that we were in Louisville, Kentucky, where tamarind trees didn't grow.

"We cut it down," I said.

My grandfather pursed his lips, his eyes still out the window, as if he couldn't trust the scenery to stay in place. These were the hardest times to witness, when it seemed as though he were teetering at the edge of his fantasies. I hated the thought of him looking down, tumbling headlong into grief.

"The tree is gone," I said, taking his hand and squeezing it until his eyes found mine. "We had to cut it down. It's gone."

Ammu was my mom's mother. I'd never seen a picture of her as a young girl, but I assumed that she and I must have looked something alike. Before she fell sick, I'd sink kisses into her soft, downy cheeks, and afterward she would wipe my mouth, joking that her darker pigment would rub off on my skin like cheap newsprint. It was the sort of endearment that irritated my mom.

The month before, my grandmother had died of a cancer that began in her thyroid. At the time, she and my grandfather were living with my uncle in Chicago, where her doctor administered modest doses of drugs that left her weak but alive. The disease simmered for a few years, then flared through her lungs. She was buried in Calvary Cross cemetery, surrounded by gravestones bearing American names, the first among our family to be buried far from home.

My grandfather had no opinions on the matter. His Ammu wasn't dead, as far as he was concerned. Adult Ammu was waiting for him to return to her, somewhere in the future, if only he could find his way back there.

My mom thought that if we kept denying my grandfather's claims about time travel, he would regain his good sense. My dad and I weren't so sure. I liked that my grandfather preferred me over everyone else in the house. I thought it funny that he was shy and polite around my parents, whom he considered his in-laws. And for the most part, he took care of me just fine while my parents were off at work. He walked me to and from the schoolbus stop and made cucumber sandwiches, sliced into tiny triangles, because Ammu took pleasure in delicate, Anglophilic things, like tea bags and butter cookies in fluted paper cups. I hated those crumbly cookies, but I ate them just to please him, and when they were finished, I got to keep the royal blue cookie tin.

·

One thing my parents and I could agree on was *The Cosby Show*. Every Thursday at 7:55 p.m., I bellowed through the halls, *"Cosby Show, Cosby Show!"* and took up my cross-legged post before the television. In the old days, my dad would plop onto the sheet-covered couch and my mom would put her feet up on his lap, just like Clair Huxtable home from a hard day's work. We'd chuckle at Theo's high-pitched distress, groan when Clair and Cliff got frisky. I enjoyed the show as much for the Huxtable clan as for the sound of my parents' laughter, though that gasping and giggling never echoed through our house anymore. Sometimes I laughed extra loud to encourage my mother's laughter, but she remained silent, her feet on the floor, her chin in her hand, as if the show were something to endure.

My grandfather never joined us for *The Cosby Show*. He mostly ignored the television because he hated sitting in any one place for too long. But one evening, just as the show began, he hovered over me and dangled a plastic bag in front of my face. I tried to peer around it. I wanted to study the opening dance sequence and learn Rudy's move.

"Ammu." My grandfather gave the bag a shake.

"Amy," my mom said sharply, for my grandfather's benefit as much as mine. "Appachen is talking to you."

I gave up and looked at him. Beaming, he dropped the bag into my lap and clasped his hands, waiting for me to open it.

Inside the bag was the pink top of a box, a bubblegum pink that seized at my heart, the pink of mini-pumps and mini-hairbrushes and all things palm-sized and perfect.

"What is that?" my dad asked.

My grandfather answered but didn't take his eyes off me. "Just a gift for Ammu. An early birthday gift."

"Amy's birthday was three months ago," said my mother,

in her patient but firm voice. I wasn't listening. I was staring at my gift, a brown-skinned Dream Glow Ken, set against a purple backdrop studded with stars. His skin was the smooth hue of Ovaltined milk. His hair was a thick, stippled helmet of black. Painted bushy eyebrows. An oyster-gray tuxedo. A pink bow tie. A sparkly vest and corsage, both of which allegedly glowed in the dark. I felt the urge to run away with him to the nearest, darkest closet.

"Is he black?" my dad asked.

"He's brown," my grandfather said while I plucked at the lid. "There were so many of the brown ones left, and they were half the price of all the others. Is this the one you wanted, Ammu?"

"Don't open that, Amy." In seconds, my mom was towering over me. "You told Appachen to spend his money on this?"

I looked to my dad for help, but he was frowning. I concentrated on the ancient scar beneath my mom's thumbnail, from where a boy once slammed a door on her hand, a mark that spoke of wild, reckless times, a life long left behind.

"I didn't tell him," I said. "I implied."

She snatched up the Ken and asked my grandfather for the receipt.

He smiled weakly, sheepish, as if he'd been scolded. "I can't buy Ammu a gift? It's my money."

"You shouldn't waste it on things like this, Pappa. The taxi alone must've been a fortune."

"I didn't take a taxi."

"Then how did you get to the store?"

He had walked. He'd remembered the route to Toys "R" Us, having seen it on our car rides to the mall. It was really no trouble. Just seven miles of padding along the highway in his lavender robe, and seven miles back, bag in hand.

·

On Monday morning, I wanted to tell Newt what had happened with Brown Ken, but he wasn't sitting in front of me. Usually I spent all ten minutes of homeroom talking with Newt, who would twist around in his seat to complain about the psoriasis on his elbows or his sister's retainer, which she'd leave on his pillow just to torture him. No one took any notice of our conversations. The girls found him too slight and pale to be cute, and the boys found him irrelevant because he couldn't catch a football. Newt had no use for them either.

Since last Thursday, times had changed. Newt had called my grandfather a jerk, and Cotillion was shaking up our social order.

From what I'd gathered, Cotillion was a cult where girls wore floral Laura Ashley dresses and learned how to curtsy and dance with boys in neckties. Newt had sworn to me that he'd never join Cotillion. He called it White People 101, which wasn't altogether accurate since Eric Madembo had joined, but Mrs. Madembo made him join everything.

That day, in homeroom, I learned that Newt had attended a Cotillion class over the weekend.

Somehow, in that one class, Newt had gained not only friends but female fans. In the hallway, a small flock of them watched as he went over the fox-trot with Betsy Warren, and I pretended not to watch from my desk. He cupped her narrow waist and steered her around, looking her right in the eye as he counted out the beats. "God, Daniel," said Lydia Coe, accompanied by a groan of such admiration and ardor, it was almost obscene. "How do you make it look so easy?" Only our homeroom teacher, Mrs. Main, called him "Daniel" or, when she was feeling chipper, "Sir Newton."

The bell rang. Newt let go of Betsy and said something that

made the girls laugh, which came as a surprise to me since
Newt wasn't all that funny in public settings. They trick-
led into the classroom. At the doorway, Lydia Coe stole the
glasses right off Newt's face and slipped them into her pocket.
She insisted it was for his own good; he looked so much better
without glasses. Betsy Warren totally agreed.

Without even glancing at me, he sank into his chair. I
thought he looked weird and planned to tell him so. "Hey," I
said. He brushed his ear with his shoulder, as if warding off a
gnat. "Hey, Newt."

He whipped around and told me it was Daniel. Just Daniel.
There was a pink, bean-shaped welt on the side of his nose.

"Sure, Newt," I said.

"Ew," Lydia said to Betsy, who was sitting to my right.
"Amy's trying to flirt."

Betsy made a gagging face. Some of the surrounding kids
turned to smirk. *Amy Abraham: flirting!* My face burned.

Fortunately, Mrs. Main clapped twice and directed our
attention to the large cardboard box in the front of the room,
beneath the chalkboard, on which was written GUATEMALAN
TOY DRIVE. Pinned to the box was a foldout poster of children
in tattered dresses and onionskin T-shirts, all dust-tousled hair
and round, raw eyes. Chris Sarmiento asked to go to the bathroom. Mrs. Main told him that he should've gone before the
bell rang. She went on to read from a brochure and pointed
from face to face: "Carlo, Cristián, José, Juan, and María."
She circled the whole gang with her forefinger. "These are our
friends from Guatemala."

We listened to her list several facts about running water,
toilets, and nutrition, each of which began with a number out
of every ten homes. I zoned out, distracted by Mrs. Main's
necklace of faded brass and wooden beads; a small gong hung
from each of her ears. She was always wearing oversized neck-

laces from other countries and twisting them thoughtfully between her fingers as she explained where each was from. She'd once claimed that she got her earrings in Mozambique, but I saw the same pair at Dillard's, and after that I felt a little sorry for her.

"So as I understand it," she told us, "we have to fill this box with toys. Dolls, games, books with not too many words. Put yourself in their shoes. What would you want?"

I tore off a corner of notebook paper and wrote, *Hey Newt. You have a weird new mole on the back of your neck. Maybe cancer.* We had learned about lethal moles in health class; I was only trying to help him out. I folded up the note and tossed it onto his desk. Lydia Coe was watching me. I bugged my eyes at her until she faced forward.

As soon as he read the note, Newt's hand shot up in the air. "Can we bring our old stuff? My sister has some Barbies . . ."

I prodded him in the back with the eraser end of my pencil.

"And a Ken," he added.

I sat back in my seat. When Mrs. Main was done with her presentation, I noisily scooted my desk and chair a few inches away from Newt's, until Madeleine Peelle, behind me, complained that my braid was getting all over her desk.

At dinner, I distilled the necessary information for my mom— the Guatemalans, the dirty water, the infant deaths, the toys. "Toys?" she said, grimacing as she poured a pot of boiled rice into the colander. "They don't have proper food and clothes, and you want to give them toys?"

I was still mad at my mom for kidnapping Brown Ken, but she didn't seem to notice. After last week's *Cosby* episode, my dad had stopped by my bedroom with a bowl of strawberry ice cream and told me to be nice to Mom because she was having a hard time. She had, in a way, lost both her parents at once. But it was tough being around my mom and the toxic sadness that trailed her all day. Whole hours went by with her supine on the bed, listening to a bland channel on talk radio. When I wandered in and asked what she was listening to, she always said, "I don't know, some trash." She continued to lay there, her forearm over her eyes, as if her brain were receiving a necessary transfusion of thought.

After that conversation with my dad, I resolved to be nicer to her. But sometimes she made it impossible, like now, by suggesting that I donate Brown Ken to the Guatemalan Toy Drive. "Appachen can't find the receipt," she said.

"*My* Ken? Why can't I have him?"

My mom handed me four plates to put on the table. I stood there, glowering, panicky, plates in hand. Steam curled up around her as if she were casting an evil spell in the sink.

I went to the table, where my grandfather was already seated, and plopped down three plates. "Easy, easy," he said, even though the dishes were plastic.

When my mom came over with the pot of rice, my grandfather raised a finger to speak. "I could buy a different doll for her to give the school."

"Don't waste more of your money, Pappa. Amy is too old for these toys."

I reasoned, as I had many times before, that the Barbie box said "5 & Up," a limitless upper limit she refused to understand. Getting no reply, I said, "You just want everyone to be in a bad mood because you're always in a bad mood."

My mom paused before ladling rice onto my grandfather's plate. I wondered if I had hit upon something true, but rather than waste time trying to pick it apart, I focused on what I understood: I wanted my Ken.

I slid down in my seat until I was eye level with the table.

"Ammu," my grandfather said quietly.

"Sit up," my mom ordered.

"I hate rice," I said. "Every day: rice, rice, rice."

"Shut your mouth." My mom grabbed my shoulder and yanked me into a sitting position.

"No, wait," my grandfather begged, laying an arm over me. "Leave her, it's okay—"

"You shut up, too!"

I stared at my mom. She had never yelled at him like that. My grandfather withdrew his hands into his lap.

"I have one child," she said, a quaver in her voice. "I don't need two."

She slapped spoon after spoon of rice onto his plate, building a hot white heap he couldn't possibly finish, then stuck the ladle in the colander and went to her room. Moments later, I could hear water gushing from her bathroom. She always took a shower when she wanted to cry.

My grandfather picked up each grain of rice that had scattered onto the table and placed them in a neat row on the edge of his plate. I stood and spooned some rice off his plate and into mine.

After dinner, I trimmed my grandfather's nails. He sat on the edge of the tub, staring drably at the drain, while I sat on the closed toilet, newspaper spread across my lap. Normally, I prided myself on my lapidary nail-cutting style, but today I made quick work of each finger, three brisk bites and on to the next.

He sniffed the air. "I can smell the *nishagandhis*. It's the midnight hour, when they bloom."

I maintained a pointed silence. All I smelled was a plug-in air freshener.

"Why am I here?" he asked the drain. His hand began to rattle in my own. His was flat and pale, limp as a glove. "Your mother never liked me. That's no surprise. I just wish I had some other place to go."

I wanted him to stop, for once. Dinner had left me shaken and guilty. I picked up a shard off the floor, a thick gray crescent. "There is nowhere else to go," I told him.

"Except down the drain. Remember?" I didn't respond. "Oh, you never remember. Should I explain it again?"

He blinked at me with his small, merry eyes, so much like my mother's.

"I know where you can go," I said in English.

It always unnerved my grandfather when I spoke to him in English. His smile faded and his face grew cloudy. His eyes moved from left to right across my face, as if he were trying to read my features.

"To a nuthouse," I said. "That's where you belong."

He looked away. He began cracking his knuckles, methodically, up one hand and down the next, wincing as if he were causing himself pain, which filled me with a different sort of pain, awful and eviscerating, that helplessness.

I clapped my hands over his knuckles. "Okay, it's okay. Tell again about the drain."

He took up where he'd left off, mostly repeating the details he'd already told me many times before. I cradled his hand and finished the rest of his nails.

In homeroom, Mrs. Main sorted through the Toy Drive box and singled out the gifts she liked best: the seven-piece tea set, the pair of badminton racquets, the plastic sewing machine that punched yarn through paper. She dangled a silver pistol between two fingers and called it "inappropriate."

I was half-hoping that Mrs. Main would call my gift "inappropriate" too, and that she would return it to me as she had returned the toy gun to an indignant Randy Porter. Instead she deemed my donation "excellent." She said it was thoughtful of me to gift the children with an ethnic doll.

Of course I wasn't planning to leave Ethnic Ken in the Toy Drive box. I thought about sneaking in during recess or getting a detention, pulling off the heist, and keeping him under my lint-ridden bed for all eternity. What could I do to get a detention? Walk barefoot to the bathroom? Say *shithead* with the authority of an eighth grader? Public disobedience didn't come easily to me, like a side ponytail I couldn't really pull off.

I was still hatching plans when Newt twisted around and whispered, "Which part of him glows in the dark?"

"His Afro," I said.

"Really?"

"No. Just his vest."

Newt grinned, paused in a way that seemed to mean he was sorry. I knew Lydia Coe was giving me massive amounts of stink eye, but I couldn't help smiling privately at my desk. That was how much I missed him.

By recess, Newt had abandoned me again. I sat on the front step of the kindergarten building, at the top of a tall concrete flight of stairs, trying to concentrate on my library book, *Amazing Myths from Around the World*. I kept eyeing Newt in the distance, merenguing on the asphalt with his little fan club. It was hard not to watch. Even Mrs. Main came over, arms crossed, impressed. He glided from step to step, his feet always moving but his face relaxed, twirling a girl behind his back or looping her arms over his head—flirty, surprising moves. The girls always looked a little stiff, smiling anxiously as if trying to guess his next step, but Newt seemed to discover the dance as he went along. They kept time to the Gloria Estefan music pulsing from Lydia Coe's mini-stereo.

Lydia Coe was bopping along, off the beat. At one point, she released her ponytail, flipped her head over, and gathered up her hay-straight hair into an even higher ponytail—one of those elegant, thoughtless gestures that I'd never be able to make with my own fuzzy curls. The other day, I'd heard her in the bathroom with Betsy, saying that Daniel was super close to asking her out. I wanted to tell her that her calculations were off by miles.

At some point during his dance, I caught Newt's eye, then went back to scanning "Loki's Quarrel." I tried to look engrossed in Loki, whoever he was.

At some point, Newt climbed the stairs and asked what I was reading. I clapped the book shut. "Nothing."

He sat down beside me. We watched the flock of girls he had left behind. They were still shuffling around, using each other as partners, not one of them as natural as Newt. "I can teach you, if you want," he said.

"I dunno. Salsa isn't really my thing."

"Merengue," he corrected me.

I rolled my head around my neck, like my mother did when annoyed. "How can you dance so long with Lydia Coe? She smells like a coconut."

"Coconut lime verbena. It's a body spray."

"I bet she can't do the Running Man."

"Can you?"

I shrugged like it was no big thing and picked at some pebbles between my feet. I could see him smirking out of the corner of my eye. "So who came up with Cotillion anyway?"

"I don't know. It sounds French."

"Like French people know about dancing," I said.

"They probably know more than you."

As he got up and walked away, I pitched a pebble down the stairs. "Yeah, well, you look like a total fruit out there."

At the top of the steps, he turned. I'd gone too far. My words cut close to the truth or what I had always perceived might be the truth. Last year, someone had penciled *Fag Newton* on the back of his chair, and I'd erased it, hoping he hadn't seen.

"At least I don't play with dolls," he said loudly.

"I don't play with dolls. I collect them."

But Newt was on a roll. He raised his voice to a yell. "And at least I have friends! All you have is your crazy grandfather!"

I dropped the book and charged at him; he raced down the stairs. Halfway down, he tripped and fell forward, rolling the rest of the way in two or three thuds. I stopped on the stairs. Newt was no more than a crumple at the bottom, his cheek against the concrete, his foot at an odd angle. I couldn't move.

Newt twitched, whimpered. I hurried the rest of the way down. He shifted, just slightly, and told me to go get someone.

I sprinted across the grass, past some of the girls, who were already running toward him. Lydia Coe shrieked above them all: "Amy, what did you *do*?" Hot tears streamed down my cheeks. I yelled for Mrs. Main, who, in her cowrie necklace, seemed suddenly a savior. With one glance at me, she started jogging in my direction, her shells chattering like teeth.

"Newt," I hyperventilated, pointing. "Fell down the stairs."

She uttered one word with total control—"Where"—and sprinted toward the crowd of girls, pumping her arms, as unaccustomed to running as I was to merengue.

I watched from a careful distance. By the time Mrs. Main

knelt down beside Newt, Lydia Coe was helping him sit up. His mouth was moving. He was telling them what had happened, how I'd raged at him like a rabid animal. Or maybe he wasn't. No one looked my way.

I went inside and put my head down on my desk, exhaling frothy rings of vapor onto the Formica. My head felt tight and clogged. Through the window I could see Newt limping along, flanked by two boys, Mrs. Main, and several more girls helping shepherd him across the grass. It wouldn't be long before Lydia Coe would come bursting through the double doors in search of ice packs. For now, it was just me and Ethnic Ken, stuck straight up in the pile of toys. The possibility of theft flashed and faded. It had never occurred to me that I could grow out of Ken in a matter of minutes, that "5 & Up" had a ceiling after all, and running straight into it left a lasting bruise.

That night, I hovered in the doorway of the bathroom. My grandfather was squatting over the drain, probing each hole with a toothbrush whose bristles were splayed and gray. "I can't get it clean," he said. He dropped the toothbrush and folded his arms over his knees, shaking his head. "I can't, I can't, I can't."

I sat on the ledge of the tub. Before he came to live with us, the tub was always speckled and laced with grime. Now it was a spotless, astonishing white, even the veins between the tiles scraped clean.

He put his face on his forearms.

"Look." I dangled a red mesh bag of marbles in front of him. I'd felt a little guilty about lifting the little bag from the Toy Drive box, but those kids weren't the only needy ones.

He drew a quick, ecstatic breath. "Where did you find them, Ammu?"

"Somewhere under my bed."

I expected him to question the label, which read, "Classic Marbles, $2." Instead, his hand closed around the bag, clenched as tightly as every tale my grandmother had told him. "See, I remembered," he said. "I remember everything."

I tore open the bag and emptied them into his palm. He fingered the different marbles—blues, yellows, reds, and clear ones ribboned with white—each a precious, painted planet. I rested my hand on his shoulder.

"It's hard, Ammu." His chin trembled. "It's hard being here."

I nodded and took the big cloudy blue from his hand, rolled it between my fingertips. I asked him to show me how to play.

Light & Luminous

...

Minal Auntie didn't sleep last night, imagining the moment she would be called to the stage and handed the trophy that has eluded her for the past four years. But now, as the competition wears on and one routine follows another, she grows drowsy. Her eyelids feel leaden. Next to her, a mother slings a towel over her shoulder and begins breast-feeding her baby beneath it, a bored look on her face.

Minal Auntie leans away from the suckling sounds and opens the program. She finds her school—"Illinois Academy of Indian Classical Dance"—and beneath it: "Minal Raman, director." Her girls are up next.

Every year, Minal Auntie ponders whether to withdraw her students from the All-India Talent Showcase, an annual event that is thick with Indians and thin on talent. In her opinion, there are far too many routines featuring untrained folk and "fusion" dancers, like the six girls currently taking up space on the stage, shimmying and writhing to a tabla-laced rap song. Last year Minal Auntie complained about a similarly indecent number whose song included the lines "He fills my cup. / I like it rough." To no avail. The worst part is watching tubby little Sanjali Kapoor thrust her hips this way and that, utterly unconvinced by her own sex appeal.

For the past two years, the trophy for Best Group Dance has gone to Twinkle Sharma of Little Star Studios. When Little Star opened three years ago, Minal Auntie predicted a quick and happy collapse; who needed a teacher for raas and bhangra and Bollywood when one could so easily mimic those dances from movies or cousins? Somehow, Little Star swelled with more students every year, all of them deluded by Twinkle's oft-repeated claim to having danced in Bollywood movies with the likes of Madhuri and Sri Devi. Whole legions have danced with Madhuri and Sri Devi, if "behind" is the same as "with."

At last, the belly dancers scuttle into the wings. After a dramatic pause, Minal Auntie's thirteen girls file across the stage, hands tucked at their waists, their *ghungroo* jingling at their ankles. Minal Auntie sits up and buries her hands in her lap.

First the girls do *namaste,* ceremoniously apologizing to the earth for the mistakes of their feet, touching fingertips to floor to eyelids. The gilded pleats of their costumes blossom open when they bend, close as they rise with their palms pressed together. They stand straight, knees locked, and wait. A few cheerful screams shoot through the dark: "Pinky! . . . Reshma! . . . Aarti!"

Aarti is Minal Auntie's grandniece, a new student, and the worst in the class. Minal Auntie can pick her out of the group at a glance: a dark, big-boned girl who copes with her size by slouching. Such a shame, to be born that dark. Minal Auntie knows, because she is equally dark, the black-brown of tamarind, a hue that surpasses the spectrum of foundation colors sold at Walmart, even those under the brand called Nubian Queen.

But this is where the similarities end; Aarti has no grace, no confidence, no future on the stage. Her mother still maintains the belief that somewhere in the twisted ladder of her little girl's DNA are the traits of a dancer. "What she needs is encouragement, *chachy*," said Lata to Minal Auntie, leaning on a term of endearment she employs in times of need.

So to appease her niece, Minal Auntie has positioned Aarti in the front and center, just for the opening of the dance. It is the simplest section of the whole routine, the part they have drilled the most.

From five rows away, Minal Auntie can see Aarti's pleats all atremble.

The girls begin the *jatiswaram* with only their necks ticking from side to side. To Minal Auntie's great relief, every neck is on point, not one lazy neck among them. The girls open their arms, palms stiff and arched. All right arms move like the oars of a mighty ship, circling the air to the held note of a woman's voice. Thirteen left arms sweep another circle with equal precision.

Soon enough, the ship breaks down. Twelve of the girls gather speed along with the beat, their gazes following the motions of their hands, their feet striking out and stamping to a single rhythm. Aarti is obeying the same rhythm, but with steps that belong to a later sequence. At first, it seems that her peers are her backup dancers, and she has come up with a solo of her own. She soldiers on, her eyes kohl-lined and blank, her lips a wide, terrified smear of red.

Pinky mutters something at Aarti, who looks over her shoulder and slows, like a robot powering down, then falls in step with the rest. By now, her smile is long gone. Minal Auntie knows the feeling: there is no lonelier place in the world than where Aarti is standing now. The girls disperse into the next formation, and Aarti shuttles to the back, where she will remain for the rest of the dance.

At home, Minal Auntie maps out the formations of the next dance she will teach to her class, for the India Day Festival two months from now. She pencils X's and O's on a yellow legal pad and intricate arrows between them. One of the O's is underlined. Every X and O has a chance in the front, except for the <u>O</u>, who will enjoy one brief moment in a middle line but otherwise will be relegated to the back. This <u>O</u> is Aarti.

Had Minal Auntie known that Aarti was the sort of student who needed underlining, she would have placed her in the beginner class. But Lata claimed that her daughter had attended a number of excellent dance camps in Ohio, under the auspices of some midwestern charlatan who refused to teach her students the proper names for each hand gesture. Instead of *Pathaka*, *Alapadma*, and *Katakamukha*, Aarti calls them Flat Hand, Flower Hand, and Deer Hand. She has never learned to hold her knees out when she bends them; after only a minute of *aramandi*, her knees cave in. At the school where Minal Auntie trained as a girl, Aarti's calves would have suffered enough raps to mottle them black and blue.

"That's terrible," Lata says when Minal Auntie brags about her old bruises and blisters. "Thank god we don't live in Chennai."

Lata utters these remarks and frowns at her watch, disappointed, as always, by the time. She has just arrived to pick up Aarti from dance class, but already she has to run. In fact, it is rare for Lata to enter the house at all; she usually beeps and waves from her minivan as the door slides shut behind Aarti. But today Lata has a favor to ask: Can Minal Auntie babysit Aarti two afternoons a week? Lata is taking an income tax course and doesn't want to waste ten bucks an hour on a babysitter.

"I don't know," Minal Auntie hedges, "I'm very busy these days."

"Oh, if you have another class, she'll sit upstairs and read or something."

Minal Auntie plucks at the frayed edge of her sari pallu. "I am in a book club. We get together in different-different houses. Members only."

"A book club?" Lata's eyes grow round and curious. "With who?"

Lata asks question after question, which Minal Auntie deflects with short answers. (Neighbors . . . Weekly . . . Whatever Oprah suggests.) "That's wonderful," Lata says, with a cloying delight that barely hides her disbelief. Just to end the conversation, Minal Auntie agrees to Tuesdays and Thursdays.

The most popular magazines at Foodfest are the ones that offer help. The experts grin from every cover, beaming with the belief that anyone can drop fifty pounds or build their own patio or achieve a positive outlook. Minal Auntie turns her back on her register and clutches her arms against the chill gusting from the air conditioners. In passing, the manager taps his own name tag, BILL, and lifts his eyebrows expectantly. She takes the button out of her pocket and pins it to her red Foodfest smock, just above her own name tag. AM I SMILING? the button reads. IF NOT, YOU GET HALF OFF.

There is little to smile about at Foodfest, where the automated registers are always beeping with customers eager to scan and bag their own items. Half the time, they jab the wrong buttons and stand there bleating for help until Minal Auntie comes to the rescue.

The cashiers have been reduced to two per shift. Minal Auntie usually finds herself paired with Krista, a black college student with the flawless air of a pageant queen, every hair slicked flat and in place. Even her eyebrows are perfect. "I get them threaded at Devon Avenue," she says, when Minal Auntie asks if she plucks. "How come you don't go to them? That's your people."

"Where is the time?" Minal Auntie says. Truthfully, she could care less about threading. Bushy eyebrows are the least of her problems.

Yesterday evening, another student quit her school in favor of Little Star Studios. Over the phone, Mrs. Tajudeen had babbled on and on about the "fun and frolic" in folk dance. "Your *bharata natyam* classes are becoming too serious for Tikku!" she chided lightly, while Minal Auntie paced the small square of her linoleum kitchen floor. She came close to confessing everything if only to hold on to one more student—how she had trouble making her mortgage payments last year, how she was forced to find a second income, how the employment agency had deemed her unskilled.

Now here she is at Foodfest, a half hour away from her home, a safe distance from the friends and acquaintances who would never guess what she has become. She punches numbers in the register and shoves the cash drawer closed when it lunges out at her. She tries to avert her gaze from the lunch station opposite, where headless chickens in a glass coffin are spinning torpidly on spits. Directly above the coffin is the clock, which moves even more slowly. After work, she will have to speed all the way back and pick up Aarti.

Krista unscrews a small gold tin of lip gloss and holds it out to Minal Auntie. "Try this. It'll look good on you."

Minal Auntie frowns. "It makes your lips look wet."

"That's the point. It's called *Wet*slicks."

Out of boredom, Minal Auntie dabs some balm over her lips. "I'm probably too old for those things."

"How old?"

"Forty-eight." Minal Auntie smacks her lips together. "So? How is it?"

"Sexy," Krista says, working her eyebrows up and down. She hands Minal Auntie a compact from her purse. In the little round mirror, Minal Auntie's lips look glazed with Krispy Kreme frosting.

"Right?" Krista says.

Minal Auntie nods. When Krista isn't looking, she wipes her lips against the back of her hand, leaving a gooey streak of glitter.

Minal Auntie screeches up to Aarti's house and beeps twice. Lata and Aarti tumble out the door, Lata bolting for her car with a hasty wave in Minal Auntie's direction. "Sorry, Auntie! Can't talk, I'm late!" Before Minal Auntie can apologize, Lata has shut the door of her minivan.

Aarti climbs into Minal Auntie's car with a laminated library book on her lap, her finger holding her place. Her face looks ghostly pale, as if covered in a film of dust, a different color from her throat. "What happened to you?" Minal Auntie asks.

"Nothing," Aarti mumbles defensively. She cracks open her

book and doesn't look up. The car has filled with the scent of Pond's talcum powder, and though Minal Auntie is sure that its source is sitting next to her, she hasn't the energy to question the girl. For the past thirty minutes, Minal Auntie has been gripping the wheel, weaving and speeding to get here. Now she feels drained, distant from the world reeling past her window, a chicken spinning around on a stick.

"Does it look bad?" Aarti asks suddenly.

Minal Auntie blinks at her; the world draws focus. She tries a tactful approach: "You don't look like you, *raja*." She gives the girl a sideways smile, but Aarti is squinting at something on Minal Auntie's shoulder.

"What's your button say, Auntie?"

Minal Auntie glances down at the thing. How did she pin it to her sweater when she has always, always pinned it to her smock? Next time she sees Bill, she will pin it to his forehead. "I found it on the ground. I liked the message."

Aarti leans in to read it. "Am I smiling . . . ?"

"Let's stop at the IndoPak store. Do you like eating *idli-sambar*?" Aarti begins a polite refusal, while Minal Auntie wrenches the pin from her shoulder so hastily she knows she's pulled a thread.

Like a pro, Minal Auntie enters at one end of the IndoPak Grocery and snakes her way up and down the dusty aisles without once doubling back, filling her jute bag with masalas, chai powder, and *masoor dal,* until she reaches the produce section, where no bruise or tenderness escapes her appraisal of okra. She arrives in the last aisle, the toiletries section, to find Aarti with a box of Light & Luminous in her hand.

Minal Auntie knows the commercial. Two girls, one fair-skinned and one nut-brown, go to a perfume counter. Brown

Girl catches her reflection in the mirror and looks away with the disappointment of a girl forbidden to play outside. Fair Girl confides that her own skin used to be similarly afflicted until she tried Light & Luminous. The commercial shows a brown patch of skin, its brownness lifted away in a whirlwind of flaky debris to reveal a paler shade beneath. Sometime later, the two girls joyfully reunite at the perfume counter, their skin so china white one can hardly be distinguished from the other.

"What do you want with that?" Minal Auntie asks.

Aarti looks up with a nervous laugh. "Do you think it works?"

"It's all chemicals. Put it back."

Aarti obeys but not without one last glance at the name on the box. She follows Minal Auntie through the checkout counter, helps carry the bags to the car, and says nothing until they are halfway home.

"A kid at school started calling me Well Done," Aarti says. "I asked him why, and he goes, 'Cause your mom left you in the oven too long.'"

Aarti plucks at the laminated plastic of her book. Minal Auntie can think of nothing to say.

"I'm not saying I wanna be super pale. I just want, you know, a normal color."

Minal Auntie studies the road for a while. At last, she says, "Your color is your color. There is nothing to do about it." She speaks from a place of impatience and experience, having wasted years on a similar quest for an antidote. She has smeared the skin of boiled milk onto her cheeks; she has stirred pinches of gold dust into her tea. When she was a child, a neighbor boy, Velu, insisted that if she stood outside at night, he could see only her teeth and the whites of her eyes.

For a moment, Minal Auntie feels these secrets on the brink of release—the milk skin, the desperation, the sound of Velu's voice in her ears—but a pickup truck in front of her brakes suddenly. She honks. The moment is gone.

Class begins as always, students trickling through the sliding door at the back of Minal Auntie's basement. They shuck their shoes outside. They knot their shawls around their waists.

Minal Auntie is seated directly in front of the mirrors with a wood block and a stick in her hands, next to an electronic box that makes harmonium vibrations. The harmonium box, the block, and the stick are the most hallowed objects in the room. Once, when the stick fell out of Minal Auntie's hand and Niva Patel absently toed it back to her, Niva was ordered to sit out the next three exercises.

After Minal Auntie pounds the block three times, the girls do *namaste,* a girl in the back sloppy in scooping forgiveness from the carpet. Afterward, Minal Auntie balances her stick on the block and instructs everyone to be seated. She can always pick out the naturals by the way they hold themselves even in unaware moments, how they stand with their shoulders back, their spines at attention, feet turned out. Overdoing it, Pinky Shahi sinks to the floor with one knee propped up, mimicking a movie courtesan. The graceless ones, like Aarti, collapse and hunch against the walls.

Minal Auntie stands to demonstrate the next sequence in the dance she has been teaching them, set to a *bhajan* celebrating the devotion of the poet Meerabai to Lord Krishna. Departing from her usual routines, Minal Auntie has choreographed a dance that contains an elaborate drama as its centerpiece, a tale of devotion, poison, and miracle.

There are only four roles—the beautiful Meerabai, her husband the cruel king, and two servants. To show the drama in its entirety, Minal Auntie inhabits all four roles, twirling between avatars. First she is Meerabai fingering her sitar, swaying in ecstatic worship to Lord Krishna, whom she considers her true husband, much to the irritation of her living husband, the king. Then she is the king, spying on his wife's worship, curling the corner of his mustache between two fingers before stalking away to his rooms. He stirs poison into a bowl of warm milk and summons his two servants. With a spin, Minal Auntie inhabits the servants, who come to the king, bowing; he points the bowl in Meerabai's direction. They bring the bowl to her. Finally, Minal Auntie is Meerabai, setting her sitar aside. Sensing that her death lies in the bottom of the bowl, Meerabai takes it and looks to the heavens, in fear not of death but of a lifetime of worship cut short. She drinks the poison, and by the intercession of Lord Krishna, she rises, immune to pain, vivified and radiant.

"Okay?" Minal Auntie says, herself again, hands on hips.

"Auntie, that was *so good*," Pinky says, the other girls rallying around with affirmations of "Yeah" and "Really good." "Who gets to be the queen?"

Minal Auntie assigns the roles: Pinky as the king, Neha and Niva as the servants, and—she braces herself for an uprising—Aarti as Meerabai.

The girls look back and forth between Minal Auntie and Aarti, as if to decode the silent conspiracies of blood relations. But Minal Auntie can't very well explain to them that there is no footwork involved in the Meerabai role, no strict rhythm to obey, and that she will never hear the end of it from Lata if she doesn't give Aarti a brief, easy moment in the limelight. "Really?" Aarti says, without much gratitude, hugging her knees to her chest.

"What about the rest of us?" asks Nidhi Kulkarni. "Where do we stand?"

"In a semicircle around the actors. Posing as Krishna."

Making a reed flute of her hands, Minal Auntie sweeps the room with a meaningful gaze. "You are all Lord Krishna."

They stare at her dully.

Nidhi rests her chin in her hand and Reshma picks at her fingernails, but the protest goes no further. Most likely it will carry on once they stuff their feet into their sneakers and shuffle away without tying their laces.

Today, for one day only, Foodfest has put a coupon in the Sunday circular for a sale on plantains—two pounds for the price of one. In the bottom left corner of the coupon, in tiny letters, are the words "Only applicable at the Downers Grove Foodfest." Additionally crippling to Minal Auntie is the fact that South Indians know at least five ways to consume a plantain: raw, fried, curried, breaded, and steamed.

And so her secret life at Foodfest has come to end.

Mrs. Namboodiri, Mrs. Markose, and Dr. Varghese are among the many Indian acquaintances who inch past Minal Auntie's cash register that day. They give her, along with their plantains, looks of surprise masked in cheery greeting.

"My cousin," Minal Auntie keeps saying. "He owns this place."

They pretend to believe her. Dr. Varghese pats the back of her hand. Each pitying smile is a blow to her heart.

Though she keeps her head down and focuses on the conveyor belt, Minal Auntie cannot ignore the tinkling babble of bracelets that can only belong to Twinkle Sharma.

At first, Twinkle places item after item on the belt without seeming to notice her cashier. They are barely acquaintances but mutually compliant with certain rules of competition, which demand that they speak warmly to each other, like old, intimate friends.

"Good price on the plantains," Minal Auntie says.

Twinkle stands there, staring, her fingers still wrapped around the handle of a milk jug. "What's this . . . ?" The question trails off as Twinkle glances down at Minal Auntie's name tag.

"I am here part-time."

Twinkle hesitates. "Okay, great!" She places the milk jug on the belt with care. "And how is your school?"

"Great." Minal Auntie takes the milk and slides the bar code over the red light, sliding it again and again until it beeps. "We will miss Tikku."

"Yes, she came to see me. Tikku has excellent form." In earnest, Twinkle adds, "You taught her well, Minal."

"I had her from when she was small."

"I know. She's always saying, 'But, Twinkle, that's not the way Minal Auntie does it!'"

"You let them call you Twinkle?"

Twinkle shrugs. "I just want them to feel comfortable with me. So they won't be intimidated when we share the stage."

"Share what stage?"

"Ah!" Twinkle smacks her forehead. "Stupid me. It was supposed to be a surprise."

"You are the teacher. How can you be in the dance?"

"It's okay, Minal."

"But there must be a rule against a teacher being in the dance—"

"I didn't have a choice. One of my girls dropped out, and we needed an even number, so . . ." Twinkle waves away all concern. "It's nothing to worry about."

Taking a bag in each hand, Twinkle remarks on how wonderful it is, running into each other. She clicks away in silver slingbacks, her heels pumiced smooth, her soles soft and uncallused, her toenails pale pink. Those are not the feet of a dancer, Minal Auntie decides, a thought that brings little comfort. She fingers a wedge of lemon she keeps in a plastic cup by her register, to mask the scent of money on her skin.

That afternoon, Minal Auntie installs Aarti in the master bedroom, where she can do her homework in privacy. Minal Auntie opens the curtains so the light falls thick and warm over her walnut desk. Just as Aarti settles into the chair, Minal Auntie notices the yellow sticky note on the corner of the desk (*Stay positive*, in her own handwriting) and crumples it into her pocket.

Aarti offers to work in the basement, but Minal Auntie says she will be busy choreographing the last portion of the dance. "About that," Aarti says, wiping her arm back and forth across the desk. "I'm nervous about being Meerabai. I don't think I'm up to it."

"If you practice, you can get good at the facial expressions."

"Nowhere near as good as you." Minal Auntie hovers in the doorway, suddenly reluctant to leave. "My mom told me what you were like when you were young. She said, 'When Minal Auntie danced, even the clock stopped to watch.'"

Minal Auntie stands still, absorbing those words. They seem to apply to another person altogether, not the woman who drove home from Foodfest earlier today, benumbed by heat and shame. If only, in her youth, she had known how to stand and receive a compliment, rather than ducking below it with self-effacing humility, as if her future would hold an infinite supply of praise. She chants this one in her head— *even the clock stopped to watch*—and it awakens in her a mild euphoria.

But the feeling dissolves when she descends the basement stairs and stands before the paneled mirrors. Here is her reflection: a flat nose, raisin-colored lips, eyebrows that have never seen a tweezer, and, of course, her skin. She turns her back on the mirrors.

Minal Auntie slides a cassette tape into the stereo. The tape has been re-recorded so many times that the first few sounds are the chaotic remnants of earlier songs. Abruptly the *bhajan* begins. Minal Auntie closes her eyes and taps her foot as Subbulakshmi's voice cascades across the opening notes, coursing through the cold air of the basement.

Instead of laying down steps for the ending, Minal Auntie dances through the drama portion. Whatever she did to impress Aarti, she can do better. She can inhabit the ecstasy of Meerabai at her sitar, the innocence with which she presses her hand to her heart when presented with the poison and asks, *For me?* She can be the king, can sense the hurt behind his anger when he sees his wife praying to her divine husband above. She can even give life to the servants, in whose pitying eyes Meerabai can read her own death.

Over and over, Minal Auntie rewinds the tape and practices with the single-minded purpose that served her well in her youth. Her guru noticed and invited her to perform on a two-week tour through Rajasthan and Delhi. She returned to hear from her cousin that the neighbor boy Velu had gotten engaged. "I always thought he liked you," her cousin said, and Minal Auntie blushed, several sensations blooming within her—surprise, pride, and, obscurely, hope. Thinking of Velu, from time to time she finds herself ambushed by the same emotions, but try as she might, she can barely remember his face.

Minal Auntie decides to play all four roles—the king, Meerabai, and both servants—for the upcoming competition.

"You?" Pinky blurts, crestfallen.

Minal Auntie pins her with a look of quiet authority. "Yes. Me."

The rest of the class seem a bit puzzled at first, but they carry on without complaint. Aarti is the only one beaming with relief.

Minal Auntie teaches the rest of the dance and has them practice at full tilt. When someone makes a mistake, she strikes the block, wags her stick at the offender, and starts the whole dance over again. She allows only a few minutes of rest between each run-through. Every girl slides to the floor except for Pinky, who sits in a butterfly stretch and brings her forehead down to her feet.

Halfway through practice, Minal Auntie allows a two-minute break. The girls trudge upstairs and drink cupfuls of water from the tap. Through the vent, she can hear their high, girlish chatter, mostly nonsense, until they arrive at the topic of Twinkle Auntie: "Did you see her at the Unnikrishnan party?" "The one with the halter blouse?" "She gets her saris from Benzer World." Minal Auntie listens for the word "Foodfest," and thankfully it never comes.

Minal Auntie called to quit the day before. She kept her excuses vague, suspecting that Bill would beg her to stay. To her surprise, he wished her well and asked her to return the smock. It was only after she hung up that her relief made way for dismay. He had taken the news very smoothly, so smoothly that he might have been hoping for it all these months while she worked her register, oblivious to her own expendability. She lingered by the phone, wondering if she'd made a mistake.

After dance class, Minal Auntie washes the crowd of dirty cups the girls left behind in the sink. "Who raised these children?" she asks aloud, though the only other person in the kitchen is Aarti, sitting at the table and hiding behind a book.

"I washed my cup," she says, but Minal Auntie only grunts in response.

The house used to belong to her brother, and seeing all these dirty glasses revives the old resentments that came of living with his family. He was the one who filled out her green-card application, and so in exchange, she was expected to wash up after the whole family—all those empty mugs and bowls ringed with grime. She taught dance from their basement, careful of her sister-in-law's rules: no students upstairs, all shoes outside, and private lessons for her son in Carnatic singing—or cackling in Sagar's case, which only made him a moving target after his school's talent show. A year later, Minal Auntie's brother announced that the family would be moving to Michigan. He expected her to go with them. Instead, Minal Auntie chose to rent the house until she could take over the mortgage. What a pleasure it was in those first few days after his departure, to sit in his favorite armchair and absorb the quiet hum of a house she could now call her own.

As Minal Auntie dries her hands on a towel, the doorbell rings. It is Lata, flushed and cheery, with her hands in the pockets of a sweatshirt. "*Chachy,* could I bother you for a glass of water?"

"What bother?" Minal Auntie waves her into the kitchen, offering other beverages and snacks. Lata declines them all, but Minal Auntie puts a plate of Nilla Wafers in front of her anyway. Rummaging around for clean glasses, Minal Auntie hears Aarti muttering with urgency about the amount of homework she has. "Then go sit in the car," Lata says sharply. Aarti storms away in a huff.

Lata takes the glass of water from Minal Auntie and swishes

the ice around. "So, six classes left until India Day, *chachy*. Are you nervous?"

"Oh, what is there to be nervous."

"I hear they're bringing in a politician."

"That's nothing new." Last year, the India Day Festival was introduced by a small but peppy state congressman who commended the Indian community for its many contributions in fields as diverse as literature (Tagore), mathematics (the number zero), and language (words like *pajamas* and *nabob*), then left after the first act. "I've performed for all sorts of politician-type people."

"But have you ever been on Asianet?" For the first time ever, Lata says, Asianet will be taping the competition and broadcasting the highlights worldwide. "If you guys win, it'll be amazing exposure for the school. Who knows, maybe student enrollment will go up."

"On TV?" Her stomach drops at the thought of what a television camera will mean. How it will take her picture and beam it into homes all over the world. Into Velu's home, possibly the very same one in which he grew up. What if the camera zooms in? What will it see? And who else will see her?

Lata takes a small sip of her water and says she better take off before Aarti starts honking. "But you barely drank your water," Minal Auntie says. "Take a biscuit at least." Lata makes her way down the hall, claiming that she binged on granola this morning.

At the door, Lata pulls a small, folded paper from her pocket and gives it to Minal Auntie. She opens it, bewildered. It is a check made out to Minal Raman, in the amount of three hundred dollars.

"It's no big deal, really," Lata says. "I should be paying you a lot more, what with all the hours she spends over here."

"*Podi pennae!*" Minal Auntie scolds her, half-mockingly. "I can't take money from my sister's daughter."

"Please, Auntie." Lata looks pained. She glances at her sneakers with none of her usual breeziness. It is then that Minal Auntie understands: Lata has heard all about Foodfest. This accounts for her sudden desire to pay, her new interest in student enrollment. "Really. You have no idea how much I'd have to pay for a nanny service. Plus there's the money you spend on gas—"

"Take it back." Minal Auntie speaks with the low control of an elder, Lata's elder. "I don't want your money."

Minal Auntie holds out the check between two fingers. Lata takes it and folds it twice, her head bowed like a scolded child. Minal Auntie remembers chasing Lata when she was just a baby toddling around her mother's legs, wearing a sun hat and sandals and nothing else. "I'm sorry if I . . . ," Lata says, then shakes her head and flashes a weak smile. "See you next week."

Arms crossed, Minal Auntie watches the car pull away but does not wave. She returns to the kitchen and sits at the table, trying to reactivate the elation that came of Aarti's words— *even the clock stopped to watch*. They taunt her now. The clock on the wall ticks on without pause, its noise interrupted by the occasional rattle of the icebox.

With a week until the show, Minal Auntie goes to an Indian beauty salon on Devon Avenue. She sits in the waiting area with a magazine in front of her face, sure that Twinkle Sharma will walk in at any moment and give her that same false smile of surprise and compassion. *You? Here?*

And why not? Over the magazine, Minal Auntie watches

a stylist furl a long hank of hair around a brush, twisting her wrist at the end to sculpt a soft curve. The client stares vacantly at her reflection, spellbound by what she sees.

Moments later, Minal Auntie is lying back in a barber chair while a threader attacks her eyebrows, upper lip, chin, and sideburns. Her eyebrow hairs will not go easily, the roots a torture to rip out. Minal Auntie clenches her armrests, a stray tear squeezing out the corner of her eye. The stylist continues without pity.

After this is a cleansing process of rose water and soap, the cool burn of witch hazel. At last Minal Auntie sits up and looks in the mirror, pressing her fingertips to the tender contours of her face. The thin skin beneath her arching eyebrows and the space between them, the smooth plane of her cheek. It is an improvement, and yet, not enough.

The stylist points to the cashier and says, "Pay there."

Minal Auntie musters the courage to quietly ask, "Have you heard of Light & Luminous?"

"Hah, yes, we use this in the Fairness Facial. You want to have the Fairness Facial?"

Does she? The stylist stands over Minal Auntie, hands on hips, waiting impatiently for an answer.

"Okay," says Minal Auntie.

The stylist leads her to a corner of the salon, where Minal Auntie lies back in another chair and closes her eyes. The process begins peacefully, with warm towels draped over her face. Once the towels are removed, the stylist scratches at her pores with something sharp, a process so painful that Minal Auntie forgets to ask about the toxicity of Light & Luminous. A smell of sulfur assaults her nose as the stylist spackles a cool, grainy cream across her cheeks, her jaw, her forehead. She is told to wait within that stinking mask, so she waits. She feels foolish, all these young women circling her, chattering in Gujarati as if she is of no more consequence than a potted plant.

Gradually, the bleach begins to tingle under her skin. She listens for the stylist's footsteps to return. Just when the tingle begins to burn, the stylist comes back and scrapes away the cream with a warm, wet towel.

The stylist gives Minal Auntie a hand mirror. "See?"

Her color is only a slight shade lighter, just a hint of cream to her coffee, but unmistakable. There is a glow to her face, a lively radiance from within. The stylist is nodding, the others gathering around in a chorus of wonder and affirmation. Buoyed by these voices, she believes them. Her new self has expanded to fill the frame of the old, fresh and resplendent, immune to pain.

At the India Day competition, the debris from performances past are strewn all across the dressing room floor: sprays of bobby pins and rubber bands, mirrors spattered with round red *bindis* and their sticky entrails. The air smells of waxy cosmetics and metallic aerosols. Throngs of girls fill the room, dressed in *punjabis* or *chaniya cholis* or classical costumes, except for Twinkle's girls, who wear sequined black nighties over red satin pants, their outfits as simple as their routines. Twinkle remains nowhere to be seen, perhaps sealed off in a dressing room of her own. One hour until stage call. There are always more flowers to add, more hooks and eyes to fasten, enough details to quickly whittle two hours down to twenty minutes.

Minal Auntie spends only a few minutes in the dressing room to inspect her dancers and give them last-minute tips. "Reshma and Rashmi, don't confuse left and right. Pinky, when you call to Krishna, don't make that sexy face. Backs curved. Knees bent. Fingers stiff. Okay?"

They nod mechanically, absorbing nothing but in need of her attentions all the same. She has applied every faceful of makeup, has held each of their sharp little chins in her hand while lining their eyes with kohl. They stand around her like a pack of wide-eyed marmots.

Minal Auntie tells her students to finish up their costumes, and she will return in thirty minutes to practice once more. Dismissed, the girls head to whatever space their mothers have staked out with garment bags and plastic Caboodles.

Minal Auntie slings her costume over her shoulder and climbs the fire-exit stairs. The chaos of the dressing room fades behind to a distant echo. Earlier in the evening, she had searched for a secluded space in which to change; the second-floor bathroom will do. Here the tiles are free of mildew, the mirrors clean, unlike the dressing room mirrors faintly gauzed with streaks.

She hangs her garment bag on the bathroom door and draws down the zipper, releasing a wave of cedar scent, anxiety, adrenaline. She pinches the pleats, the gold still stiff though the wine-red silk has softened with washings and wear. She fingers each deliberate stitch her mother made along the shoulder in mismatching red thread. One by one, she fastens each of six separate pieces around her body, and though some of the hooks strain against the eyes, the costume hugs her as close as it should.

Before tackling her hair, Minal Auntie drapes a towel over her chest and unscrews the tube of Light & Luminous. A week has passed since she left the salon with a brand-new face, and her old one has crept back into the mirror. She was planning to touch herself up in the morning, but with the whirlwind of bells and nail polish and *bindis,* she couldn't find fifteen minutes for herself.

She prepares the mixture, pauses, then taps in a bit more powder. Holding her nose, she frosts her face thickly. The sulfur smell fills her mouth.

As the cream sets, Minal Auntie braids her hair, injecting bobby pins. Her skin begins to tingle. To distract herself, she thinks of Twinkle. Is she wearing the same outfit as her students, black sequins and red satin, a frayed scrap of red georgette pinned over her head? A warmth prickles across Minal Auntie's skin. She draws deep breaths of air.

Before she has a chance to rinse the cream from her face, she hears the jingling of footsteps down the hall, the lazy chatter of girls. She shoves her makeup into her bag and locks herself in the handicapped stall, moments before they burst through the door.

Voices and the slap of bare, belled feet. "I told you guys there's an open bathroom," says Pinky. Minal Auntie nearly backs into the toilet, holds her breath. "We can practice in private here."

"What's this white stuff?" Rashmi says.

"Ew. It smells like pee." A pause. "What's 'Light & Luminous'?"

Minal Auntie's eyes are stinging. Waves of cold seethe across her skin.

"Dude," Pinky says. "Is this what Minal Auntie's been using?"

"No way," says Aarti. "She wouldn't touch that stuff."

"How do you know?"

"I wanted to buy some one time, but she wouldn't let me. She said it was stupid." Aarti hesitates. "She said your color is your color, and there's nothing you can do about it."

"She said it like that?"

"Whatever," Aarti says. "It's true."

Minal Auntie is jolted by the sound of her own words in Aarti's mouth, spoken with such flat resignation. It seemed, at the time, like honesty, meant to equip the girl with a tougher skin.

"Oh, please," Pinky says. "She obviously uses it. Her face looks all chalky and stuff. A facial doesn't make you look chalky. I've had them before."

"Pinky, come on—"

"No, I'm sick of this new Minal Auntie! She acts like our dance is her diva moment. She's supposed to be our teacher."

"Twinkle Auntie's dancing with her girls."

"I watched them rehearse," Pinky says. "Twinkle Auntie goes on at the end for, like, a minute, and she's in the back the whole time. She didn't make herself the star. What Minal Auntie's doing, it's . . ." Pinky falters. "It's embarrassing."

Minal Auntie waits for Aarti to defend her, but no one does.

"So should we practice or what?" Rashmi asks.

Minal Auntie can bear the stinging cream no longer. She unlocks the stall door, and aside from a few small gasps, the girls go dead quiet. She looks straight ahead as she strides to the counter. Turns on the faucet. Throws handfuls of water over her face. Gritty white dollops plop onto the porcelain of the sink.

"Auntie, we didn't know you were in there," Pinky says weakly. Minal Auntie scrubs her cheeks in slow, mechanical circles. She feels spent, as though she's been dancing for days and has nothing left. She can't go onstage, knowing what everyone thinks of her. But she must. She has made herself the star.

Minal Auntie dries off her face with a paper towel. In the

mirror, her old face looks back at her, only the slightest shade lighter than her tamarind brown. With trembling fingers, she brushes her own cheek, just as she did at nine years old, when she snuck out of her house at nightfall, the hand mirror in her fist, to see if Velu was right. And here she thought she had outgrown that little girl, had shed her like an old, dead skin.

"Auntie," Aarti says. "Are you okay?"

The gazes of the girls press against her on every side, their silence far louder than any noise they could make all together. She opens her mouth to speak, but a shiver passes through her as if she is still stranded in the middle of a night so dark, she has all but disappeared.

Escape Key

. . .

All throughout childhood, my older brother refused to jump from the high dive, a phobia for which I gave him constant hell. "Amit is a chickenshit!" I'd yell, while leaping flamboyantly off the board. At twenty-nine, he dove off the roof of his buddy's three-story condo. Later, he couldn't recall his reasons or the fifth of whiskey in his system or the ER, where he lay with his neck locked in a collar, while my dad called to give me the news: *He can't move his legs*. With my dad talking into one ear, I looked around my room. All my belongings were stuffed in a few distended boxes, words like FRAGILE and THIS SIDE UP scrawled on the sides.

I rushed to the airport, feeling oddly calm even as I shuffled from ticket desk to ticket desk, even as I sat elbow to elbow at the gate, inhaling the intimate odor of my neighbor's egg roll but lacking the will to rise and lose my seat. I opened my laptop and typed an e-mail to Katie, my roommate, asking her to post my boxes home. I wrote: *My brother had an accident. He's in the hospital.*

I hit send just as I realized that I'd sent the e-mail to the wrong Katie. I'd e-mailed Katie the bartender from Fiddlesticks, whom I'd gone out with a lifetime ago and never called back. I spent a few minutes trying in vain to un-send my e-mail. I held down the escape key, but it jammed, and in trying to jimmy it loose, I plucked it out. It lay like a tooth in my palm. That was when I closed my fist and lost it. A sudden silence piled up around me. I heard a little girl ask her mommy if I was crying. After a few moments of this, the egg roll guy gave me two of his napkins, and I blew my nose into his grease.

I'd spent the past nine months as a writer-in-residence at a private boarding school outside of Boston, where I taught a creative writing class and occasionally messed around with Caryn, the English teacher. Teaching hadn't come easily to me. For one thing, I hated most of my students, chief among them Judy Grubich, who called Mark Twain a douche for his scathing takedown of *The Leatherstocking Tales*. She couldn't let a day go by without cussing out an author I loved. I thought I'd be molding young minds, but by the end of the semester, all I had molded was one very prickly critic who would be gunning for my first book, should it ever be published.

Caryn told me not to feel bad. She said that she'd studied with some brilliant writers who were terrible teachers. "How do you know I'm not terrible at both?" I asked. She'd never read my novel, though she had casually offered to, more than once.

"Not possible," Caryn said. "You won that Prague thing."

The Prague thing: my first taste of recognition. I had submitted the opening chapters of my novel to a contest in which the winner would be flown to Prague for a two-week master class, followed by a six-month stint at an artists' colony. I didn't tell my brother or my dad about the prize. I knew what they'd say—"Did you get any money?"—leaving me annoyed and a little embarrassed.

For the time being, I was content to imagine myself in Prague, typing by pallid moonlight, stone bridges and spires out my window. I'd always lived in relatively small, static towns. Prague seemed just the place to bridge the person I was with the writer I wanted to be: traveled, ambitious, alone.

A few days after the surgery, Dr. Tehrani showed us a series of X-rays. The rods that had been planted in Amit's back looked like railroad tracks, blazing white against the ghostly outlines of his bones. "It's too early to know what functions you'll regain," Dr. Tehrani said. "We'll have to keep up with the physical therapy, take it one day at a time." In the silence after his statement, I remembered how I knew Dr. Tehrani—from my parents' dinner parties, his pouchy eyes perpetually apologetic, even when asking me, a little boy, where he should discard his paper plate.

I half-expected my dad to argue with him, as if the fact that they were both doctors could lead them to bargain down the verdict. But no one spoke. Dr. Tehrani left. My brother, my dad, and I stayed very still.

"Neel, hand me my phone," Amit said. Before long, he was deep into a game of poker. My dad stared at the blank TV screen. We were lacking the kind of direction my mother would have provided if she were alive. She would have been sobbing or interrogating a nurse or tugging me by the sleeve to the hospital chapel. My mother had been the only religious one in the family. She died when I was ten, and I was pretty sure that no one had been praying for us since.

·

Every day for three weeks, a baby-faced doctor came into Amit's hospital room and tested his limbs with an instrument that appeared to be half of a long Q-tip. The doctor had Amit close his eyes. "Hard or soft?" the doctor would say, after pressing the cottony end of the Q-tip into Amit's thigh. With every press, Amit shook his head and muttered, "I don't know. Nothing." When it was over, he'd stare at his thigh, as if willing it to tell him something.

While Amit spent those weeks in the rehab center, my dad and I prepared the house for his return. My dad shuffled his patients around and sought coverage from colleagues so he could take the next month off from work. He and I carried the living room couch to the basement and set up a twin bed in its place. He hired Diego, a longtime patient, to install grab bars in the bathroom down the hall. Beyond the price of materials and a midday beer, Diego shook his head at payment.

Once Amit came home, my dad hardly left his side. He assisted Amit in shifting between the bed and the wheelchair, using a board that Amit could scoot himself across, setting aside each loose limb as he went. He also helped Amit get situated in the bathroom. I wasn't sure what went on in there exactly, but I had an idea from the accessories along the sink: a box of latex gloves, a dented tube of lubricant. I tried not to think about it.

I'd read somewhere that pets lower blood pressure, so I went to my brother's apartment and brought back the ten-gallon tank he'd had for years, filled with fake ferns and a presiding toad named Moses. I installed the tank along one wall of the living room. Twice a week, I dangled a doomed earthworm in front of Moses's mouth, sometimes tapping his lips as if knocking at a door, before he awoke and clamped down on the head with a savagery that made me jump back.

For the most part, Amit lay in bed or sat in his rocking

recliner, as motionless as Moses. He kept the TV on, the shades drawn, suffusing the room in dim blue. Sometimes his leg bounced in place, like it had a mind of its own. On his second day, a back spasm slammed him hard enough to topple his rocker; he went so stiff with pain it hurt him to weep, even to breathe. My dad increased his Baclofen dosage, and we replaced the rocker with a heavy leather armchair.

Once, while I was trying to feed Moses, I dropped the worm on his head. It lay there like a coiled little turban, just above Moses's catatonic gaze. I looked at Amit, who had cracked a smile, the first I'd seen on his face in a long time, and for a moment, my heart rose and I forgot all about Moses. "Well?" Amit said. "Go in and get it, dumbass."

"Moses is the dumbass." I lowered my hand into the tank. "Who even has a tank anymore?"

"Do it, Moses. Eat his whole hand off."

While my brother heckled, I airlifted the worm and swung it into Moses's mouth. The ordeal was disgusting and entirely worth it, just to be ourselves again, for a little while.

There was one night when Amit fell asleep earlier than usual, at 9:00, and I went upstairs, determined to work. Or check my e-mail. Nothing special, aside from a number of lefty groups urging me to sign their petitions. I spent five minutes studying the plight of honeybees. I spent another five minutes perfecting a message to Stefan Baziak, the director of the Prague program, saying I would have to put my confirmation on hold due to a family emergency.

I scrolled through my novel and weeded out a few errant semicolons. I stuffed plugs in my ears and listened to the magnified rush of my own breathing. I fell asleep on my arm, woke up at 11:11. I made a useless wish. I went to bed.

•

In those days, Amit had one standing order: if anyone was to call or visit, he was napping. His friends took the hint and stayed away. His coworkers at Blue Grass Realty sent a potted bamboo, the stalks deformed into the shape of a heart. Only Ivy, his girlfriend, continued to call. I'd almost forgotten the stuffed-up sound of her voice, the nasal quality that made a stuttering idiot out of me. "Seems like his narcolepsy kicks in every time I call," she said.

I laughed a little too loudly. I told her he'd call her back.

"I can't believe you're still doing that," Amit said, after I hung up. "Christ."

"Doing what?"

"Your voice, when you know it's her. Your James Earl Jones impression." He lodged a cheese puff, like a tumor, in his cheek. "You sound like a serial killer."

Amit and Ivy had been dating since high school. At first, my dad didn't approve because her parents were Chinese, and he'd long held the notion that all Chinese people were calculating and aggressive, as evidenced by some decades-old invasion of India that continued to work him up. As the years went by and Ivy stuck around, she and my dad moved toward a cool détente, though it still pained him to report when an Indian person we knew had married outside the tribe. His tone would be like that of a newscaster reporting casualties— another woman lost, another man down.

I'd been sweet on Ivy since the day she asked Amit to the senior prom; that she'd done the asking suggested an alluring form of Chinese aggression. She even picked him up in her dirty white Saab, wearing a pink satin pouf that made no secret of her cleavage. "I got it at a thrift store," she said to me, doing a twirl. "Isn't it hideous?" Before I could answer,

Amit thundered down the stairs in his tux, and her face tilted up, filling with light.

I watched them speed off, thinking, *Him? Really?* I attributed her mistake to the fact that she was a transplant from San Francisco and didn't know any better. Here was a girl who could surf as well as her brothers, who sang at the talent show a sultry cover of "Oh! Darling" while strumming her own acoustic guitar. Not that I deserved her either. Ivy seemed to be on another plane of special altogether, destined for a life of big cities and backstage passes. Amit, I assumed, was a youthful detour.

A week passed, and things began to improve after I ordered a copy of *Planes, Trains & Automobiles,* a movie that Amit and I had watched so many times as kids that we knew whole scenes by heart. I usually played Steve Martin, the hapless traveler forced to cross the country with John Candy, a boisterous shower-ring salesman. Watching it again, so many years later, brought a strange sense of relief. Most of the time, I was laughing because Amit was laughing.

After the first screening was over, I wheeled Amit to the bathroom and left him in there. He visited the bathroom only two or three times a day, usually for an hour each time. It took that long for his bladder and bowels to function. I kept his bathroom stocked with issues of *Rolling Stone* and *Time,* books of crossword puzzles and Sudoku.

He'd been in the bathroom for ten minutes when I glimpsed Ivy's Saab crawling up our driveway.

"Amit?" I said through the door. "Ivy's here."

Silence.

"Amit, you okay?"

"I'm not here, got it? Tell her I'm not here."

"Where do you plan on going?"

"Don't tell her I'm in the bathroom, Neel. Tell her I'm asleep."

"That's what I always tell her. She'll know I'm lying—"

"Okay then, why don't you tell her I just stuffed a fucking suppository up my ass and I can't come out or else I might shit all over myself, huh? How's that?"

The doorbell chimed.

"I'll take care of it," I said.

I opened the front door to find Ivy standing with her hands in the back pockets of her jeans. Her hair was shorter, fringe over her eyes, which were lined and tired. "Oh, hey, Neel."

"Hey, you!" I said, regrettably.

We hugged, then stood there, nodding at nothing. She looked down at the ramp of wooden planks beneath her feet, which Diego had hammered together. "Been a while," I said.

"Yeah. Hey, how's your writing?"

"Okay, I guess." I leaned against the door frame, attempting a pose as casual as hers. "I finished a draft of my novel."

"Really? What's it about?"

"Brothers," I said. "Basically."

"Uh oh." A smile tugged at the corner of her mouth. "A tell-all, huh?"

"Not exactly." I felt a childish desire to impress her. "Actually it won an award. I'm supposed to go to Prague for this artists' colony . . ."

"You're leaving?" Her smile disappeared. "When? For how long?"

"In a couple months." I scratched at a peeling patch of paint on the door frame. I still hadn't discussed my plans with Amit, and here I was, unloading on Ivy. "I haven't decided. We'll see."

"Wow," Ivy said, but not in the tone I'd hoped for. "Good for you."

She peeked over my shoulder at the tank. Moses was on his relaxation rock, his back to both of us.

Ivy said, "Still sleeping, huh."

I shrugged, smiled weakly.

"All right, I'll go." Ivy lowered her voice. "But tell him he can't sleep forever."

She left me with a package for Amit—some PayDays, a DVD of *Sense and Sensibility*, and, oddly, a box of Darjeeling teas.

I removed the DVD. "You can probably have this one back."

"Oh no, that's his," she said. "Yeah, he loves *Sense and Sensibility*. You didn't know that?"

On Mondays, Wednesdays, and Fridays, my dad helped Amit into the wheelchair and rattled him down the ramp toward the car that would take them to physical therapy. I spent those three hours in my bedroom, trying to write. Once, I used my brother's computer and stumbled across a small, multicultural library of porn. I spent some time in the Asian division.

I also got to thinking about Caryn a lot, her bright, elfin eyes peering at me over a crappy hand of cards. She looked like a student herself, in jumpers and wool tights that rasped when she walked. Things had ended breezily between Caryn and me. She had gone home to Newton before I had a chance to tell her about my brother, and now I couldn't find the words. So instead, in a late-night moment of beery loneliness, I e-mailed her my novel.

She sent a brief and instant reply: *!!!*

I figured that Caryn would make a better reader than Amit.

He had always viewed my writing with a combination of bewilderment and dismissal, as if I were trying on a panama hat and had yet to glance in a mirror and see how ridiculous I looked. My dad told anyone who asked that I was a teacher.

Two weeks into my time at home, I called Caryn. Our conversation lurched from one piece of nonsense to the next—her new coffee press; what constitutes the ideal mug—and as the minutes gathered, my stomach began to jostle with dread.

"Well, I read it," she said, finally.

"Yeah?"

"And I jotted down some notes."

I found a pen, a notepad. "Okay. Ready."

"So the first few chapters are great." She paused. "But around page fifty or so, the story starts to sag."

I wrote: *page 50 → sag.*

"Partly because you spend all this time on describing every little thing," she continued. "And, I dunno, I'm not one for fussy prose, it's just not my thing. Like here, with the playground scene on page sixty-three: *while the four hobbyhorses, nostrils aflare and frozen, glared down on us in what seemed an apocalyptic moment.* I marked a lot of places like that, where it feels like you're trying too hard."

"Okay."

She recommended cutting a number of scenes. "The swimming pool thing, for example? Where the one brother doesn't make it up the high-dive ladder?" I heard her flipping pages. "I didn't see the point. Other than the fact that the younger brother is kind of a prick."

"I dunno, it sort of seemed to paint a picture of the relationship right away, their relationship."

"Yeah, but, it's . . ." She paused, searching for the perfect word. "Boring. Also, how come they never talk about the mom?"

"I don't know. They just don't."

This went on for half an hour. I drew a turd with a big bow on top.

In the last five minutes, Caryn seesawed her comments in the positive direction, trying to boost me with vague praise for my thorough characterization, my attention to setting, her voice full of pity and pep. By this point, I was lying on the couch.

As the conversation wound down, Caryn reassured me that the future was still bright. "It's awesome that you'll be around all those writers in Prague. Maybe one of them can give you advice."

"Yeah, maybe." I promised to write her from Prague. I could tell that she didn't believe me.

"Good-bye," I said.

"Good luck!" she said, and hung up, leaving me to ponder her word choice.

Early in the evening, Dr. Pillai stopped by with his wife. Dr. Pillai was an old friend of my dad's, a nice-enough guy with a tussock of hair growing out of each ear, which Ruby Auntie somehow seemed to ignore. She thrust three plastic yogurt containers of Indian food into my arms, though we'd all but stopped eating Indian food after my mom died. I pushed the brothy containers deep into the fridge.

We gathered around Amit like careful pilgrims, even though he was in no mood for visitors. He'd just come home from therapy, which always wrung the life out of him. He lay on the bed, propped up on pillows, staring at the muted television, where a weatherwoman gestured to a series of pulsing suns.

"The PT," my dad said, "she is tough."

"That's good!" said Ruby Auntie.

"Yeah, great," Amit said. He gazed at the weatherwoman with detached interest.

"So, Neel," Dr. Pillai said, "what are you writing these days?"

"A novel," I said, nodding. Dr. Pillai blinked at me expectantly. "About brothers."

"So a biography, then?" Ruby Auntie asked.

"Autobiography," Dr. Pillai corrected.

"No, not exactly—"

"You should tell him some stories," Ruby Auntie said to my dad, who said, "Oh yeah, definitely," as if he'd been thinking the same thing for years. "Growing up in India, things like that," Ruby Auntie suggested. "How many stories can a twenty-four-year-old have?"

"He's twenty-seven and his brother's a cripple," Amit said. "Isn't that enough?"

"I don't like that word," my dad said.

"Too bad."

My dad smiled apologetically in Dr. Pillai's direction. "He's just tired. He hasn't been sleeping well."

Amit narrowed his eyes at my dad, then lavished Dr. Pillai with a warm, toothy grin. "Yeah, I'm not used to sleeping on my side. But I have to, or else a fungus'll start growing on my balls."

I coughed, snorted orange juice through my nose.

"Fungus on your . . . ?" Dr. Pillai said.

"Balls."

"Amit," my dad said.

"What? It's true."

"See that," Ruby Auntie said, pointing at the television. "That was from last night's tornado. In Mississippi, I think."

We all fell silent for a moment, watching an old woman pick through the rubble of her home. Looking lost, she took a seat on the concrete front steps, which was the only part of her house still standing.

Dr. Pillai was the first to speak. "It does make you think."

"Of what?" Amit said.

"Whatever you are suffering, someone else is suffering more."

"I feel better already."

"That is not what he meant," my dad said. "Don't twist people's words." This was something my mother used to accuse us of, contorting her English words as though they were animal balloons.

"Uncle means that the glass is half full," Ruby Auntie offered.

"Some glasses are cracked," Amit said. "Some glasses are fucked."

Dr. Pillai scratched his furry ear and smiled desperately at me. My dad put a hand to the back of Amit's head, but Amit flinched away.

I'd only been home a month, but I missed the sultry air of a Boston summer, the ceiling fan creaking in its fixture, Caryn's limbs tangled in mine despite the heat and the threat that the fan could fall at any minute. At night, she would stand up in bed and reach for the fan's chain, her torso one moonlit length pulled taut.

But how to reconcile that Caryn with the Caryn who had gored my work the week before? I didn't have the energy to sort through her comments, most of which I'd recorded in my series of cryptic sketches. Whenever I sat down to write, I saw only detours and dead ends. I went for a jog around the neighborhood to clear my head, but ten minutes in, I popped a cramp and wound up clutching my stomach in a posture of failure made worse when a Lincoln slowed down to make sure I was okay.

The next morning, I was unloading the dishwasher when the director of the Prague program called me. "Neel, hello, this is Stefan Baziak." Mr. Baziak's voice was scratchy and womanish, eccentric and intimidating. "I hope this is not a bad time?"

I glanced into the living room. My dad was helping Amit scoot across the board and into the armchair. "No, not bad at all."

"I hate to bother you, but I am calling about the visa and the medical clearance. Were you able to file? Are you coming to Praha?"

Praha—the word sent through me a small ripple of delight. "I'm not sure yet, to be honest. Things are still sort of hectic here."

"Yes, yes, I understand. Of course, we would love for you to come. We very much enjoyed the first portion of your novel, particularly the braiding of each boy's point of view . . ."

As Mr. Baziak continued, my dad returned and opened the fridge. He removed a small crate of strawberries. He ran the faucet and rinsed them in the sink, staring at the tube of gushing water with a deadened expression.

"Dad—" Amit called.

"Yep!" Snapped awake, my dad shut the faucet and hurried over with the strawberries, dripping water as he went.

"Neel?" Mr. Baziak paused. "You're still there?"

"Yes! Thank you, thanks."

"Thank you for what?"

"For everything. For the opportunity. Excuse me—" I faked a cough. "I should have things sorted out in the next few days or so . . ."

"Because we need to know fairly soon if we must pull someone from the wait list. You can always apply again next year."

"No," I said quickly. "I mean, I'm coming. I'll look up the visa requirements tonight."

After hanging up the phone, I found my dad and Amit arguing in the living room. "Strawberries are good for you," my dad insisted. "Since when did you start hating strawberries?"

"Since forever," Amit snapped. "Don't we have any kettle chips? Jalapeño flavor?"

My dad turned to me. "Was that Ivy who called?"

"Uh, yeah. I told her Amit was sleeping."

"Why?" my dad said. "Call her back, invite her over!"

"Don't." Amit pointed the remote at the TV, increasing the volume on *Planes, Trains & Automobiles*. Steve Martin was throwing a fit in the airport parking lot, clutching at the air and cursing hysterically, hurling his suitcase at the ground. My dad looked sorry for Steve, then waved a hand at the TV and left the room.

I was leaping up the first few stairs when Amit paused the movie and called after me. "Where're you going?"

I stopped, turned. "Upstairs."

"Stay here."

"Why?"

"I don't laugh when you're not here." Amit looked at the TV. A sudden awkwardness sprang up between us. "Nothing's funny when you watch alone. It's a fact." He casually scratched his crotch with the remote.

"That's nice, Amit. Get your crotch fungus all over the channel changer."

"Are you coming down or what?"

I glanced at the clock over the TV. The ticking sounded loud and strange, almost impatient. I came down the stairs, and Amit pressed Play.

·

On Sunday afternoon, Amit and I went outside. His thera-
pist had suggested that he increase his arm and abdominal
strength by wheeling himself for a few miles. I jogged beside
him to his chosen destination, the refurbished playground by
our old middle school. The wind churned around us, jostling
the swings, the clouds a dingy gray.

Once he caught his breath, Amit removed a blue glass pipe
from one pocket and one of Ivy's Darjeeling tea bags from the
other. He undid the sachet on his knee and pinched apart a
fuzzy chunk of weed.

"Clever," I said.

He paused, as if he were about to say something sarcastic,
then changed his mind. "Yeah, she is."

"Not to ruin the mood, but I thought you're trying to build
stamina—"

"Neel, can you not, for once?"

Some time later, I was sitting on the grass, my lungs pleas-
antly seared. All of a sudden, life seemed manageable again.
I flipped my eyelid inside out, a weird pastime I'd forgotten.
"Sick," Amit said, so I flipped the other.

He sucked down the last drops of Gatorade I'd brought along
and tossed me the empty bottle. His eyes went soft and tranquil.

"Did you read that *Life After SCI* pamphlet?" Amit said.
"The hospital gave it to me."

"No."

"There was a part called Sex on Wheels."

A little voice in my head whispered: *Sex on wheels!* I gnawed
on the rim of the bottle.

"And there was a picture of this vibrator . . ." Amit sounded
half creeped out, half curious. "A vibrator for dudes."

We fell into a harrowing silence.

Amit leaned his head back, squinted at the clouds. "Dad
wants me to get back with Ivy."

"You are with Ivy."

"We broke up a few months ago."

I tried to focus my gaze on Amit. "Broke up why?"

"She wants to spend the summer in San Francisco. Grow out her armpit hair. Go lesbo for a while."

"She said that?"

"No." He turned the lighter over, studying it. "Dad thinks if I pass her up, no one else'll want me."

I heard the scratch of the flint wheel. Amit watched the flame until a breeze snuffed it out.

"Seems like Ivy wants something," I said. "She calls all the damn time."

"She just feels sorry for me. She'd get bored, eventually."

"How do you know?"

He clasped his hands over his stomach. "Well, for one thing, she's not a big fan of the rodeo. Sexually speaking. And that's the only ride I got left."

I stared at the grass until Amit said, "Stop picturing it, perv." I lay on my back. The grass felt weird and ticklish to my ears.

When I caught sight of a Saab pulling into the parking lot, I thought I was hallucinating. I heard Amit go, "Shit." Magically, Ivy emerged from the car and walked across the grass toward us, her hair pulled back from her eyes, looking exactly how she used to look, and I sat up, a familiar ache in my belly.

I realized it was the first time Ivy had seen Amit in the wheelchair. She fixed her gaze on his face, as if determined not to look elsewhere. "So you got my gift," she said.

"Yeah," Amit said. "Thanks."

"Hey, Ivy."

"Hi, Neel." She barely glanced at me. "So what's with you blowing me off all the time, Amit?" He picked something off the tip of his tongue. "I mean, shit, I'm not your groupie."

"You're not my girlfriend either."

Ivy pressed her lips together. She looked like she wanted to punch him.

He gave her a lazy smile. "Peace pipe?"

I cupped my hand around the bowl while Ivy lit up. A sense of perfect bliss billowed through me as I stood there, close to her, watching the embers pulse and fade. Her hair gave off a minty sweetness. She stepped back and coughed, spat expertly.

Amit asked her how she'd known we were at the park. Ivy said that she'd called the house, and our dad had told her. "He's been really nice to me," she said, "which is weird." Amit rolled his eyes at me, as if to say, *See?*

After a while, we went wandering into school through the gym doors, which were unlocked. The hallways were dim and smelled of kid sweat and sneakers. I stopped by a wall hung with group portraits from each year's play production. "Nice," Amit said, pointing at one of the frames: That was the year I played the title role in *Aladdin,* even though I did more yelling than singing. I stood with a huge white turban on my head, arms akimbo, in a credible portrayal of confidence. It was hard to remember being that compact. But I did remember the note our director, Miss Mott, had written me: *You're going places, kiddo.*

Someone called down the hall, "School's closed. How'd you all get in here?" We mumbled apologies and hurried back the way we came.

As I pushed Amit across the parking lot, Ivy asked me what was going on with the Prague thing.

I looked straight ahead, trying to think of another topic, but my thoughts moved like syrup. We came to a stop by Ivy's car.

"What Prague thing?" Amit said.

Ivy looked at him, then me. "You didn't tell him?"

"It's just six months . . ."

"*What's* six months?" Amit said.

"This artists' colony," I said. "To hang out in Prague and write. It's pretty prestigious." *Pretty prestigious* came out a little slurry.

Amit paused, digesting the news. "You tell Dad?"

"Not yet. I will."

"Colony," Amit said, as if he'd just learned a strange word. "I thought those were for nudists. And lepers."

"I was gonna tell you—"

"Whatever, hey. It's fine." Amit shrugged. "It's good news."

Ivy said she had to go. She paused, then kissed the top of Amit's head, a gesture that he didn't seem to enjoy, and waved at me before getting in her car. On our way home, Amit chose to wheel himself. He said he wasn't tired, but toward the end, I could hear him faintly wheezing.

During the last week in July, the temperature languished at an unbearable 102 degrees. The AC was busted, blasting the rooms where no one went, like my dad's study, and ignoring the living room entirely. My dad positioned a standing fan at Amit's feet; it spent the whole day looking him up and down. Sitting outside the fan's sweep, I crunched on cups of ice and tried to stay as still as possible.

Since that day in the park, I'd been careful around Amit. I kept him fed, made sure not to cross in front of the TV. He spoke to me only when he needed something and my dad wasn't around to provide it. He never said my name.

One evening, my dad came into the living room, holding out his wrist so I could fasten the complicated clasp of his fancy watch. He was attending a wedding reception, his first time leaving us alone at night. Before he left, he asked Amit if he needed to peepee.

"Really, Dad? Peepee?"

"No?" My dad hovered over him, twisting his watch around his wrist. He plucked a pillow feather out of Amit's hair, and for once, Amit didn't duck away.

At the door, my dad gave me three different numbers to call in case of emergency. I told him not to worry.

"So, what are you doing tonight?" my dad asked. "Going to work on your novel?"

"Oh, that. That's on hold for now."

My dad nodded. "It's good to take a break sometimes."

"Good for who?"

My dad gave a sheepish smile. "If you weren't here, he would eat me alive." He looked like a little kid, his eyes beginning to fill.

I thumped him on the back and suggested he get going before he missed cocktail hour.

After my dad left, I brought us each a Guinness from the fridge. I'd gone shopping earlier in the day and stocked up on Amit's favorite, along with more pork rinds. "You don't have to babysit me," he said, taking the bottle.

I put my feet on the coffee table. "I'm fine. I like"—I squinted at the screen, sighed inwardly—"*What Not to Wear.*"

Amit shuffled through the next five channels, barely pausing long enough for an image to appear. He settled on a commercial narrated by a talking gecko.

"Why don't we call Ivy?" I suggested.

"Do you have some kind of memory problem? I told you, we're not together."

"So, what's the big deal? She could rent us a movie."

Amit took a breath and let it out slowly. "The deal is, she's gone."

Apparently, Ivy had flown to San Francisco the day before. I didn't ask how he'd known, or what happened, or why. Maybe she'd been waiting for him to let her off the hook. Maybe all it took was *You're not my girlfriend either.* On TV, a woman was in a bathtub, drawing a loofah over her moisture-rich leg. Steam flowered up around her blissed-out smile. That day in the park seemed painfully far away.

"What about you?" Amit took a long swig, winced. "Bought your ticket yet?"

"I reserved a flight, yeah."

He studied the Guinness label. "You should tell Dad. I don't give a shit, but he will."

Amit set the bottle on the floor and lay back against his pillows, closed his eyes.

I finished my beer, and his. The TV was still on, but mostly I was staring at Moses. I'd never paid much attention to the poster taped across the back of his tank, an ethereal landscape of gold-lit trees receding into the distance. Maybe, at one point, he'd leapt into it and had the hope knocked out of him. Maybe that was why he sat there now looking the dazed way he did.

Soon, Amit was snoring. Even in sleep, the little line between his brows remained. I wondered if it would still be there fifty years from now. I wondered if the chair cushions beneath me would mold to my shape. I imagined the two of us watching the same movies over and over, not because they were still funny but because they reminded us of who we used to be. I'd grow bitter, encumbered by the inventory of all I'd failed to do. Or worse, I wouldn't care.

When the show was over, I trudged upstairs.

I thought maybe I'd soak in the bathtub for a while, like

the loofah commercial, minus the loofah. I wanted something cleansing and cool and quiet. I wanted to come up with a way to tell my dad that I was leaving.

I poked around in the potpourri basket over the toilet and found a bottle of lavender bubble bath solution, probably my mom's. Two capfuls turned the tub into a bed of sudsy white. The room filled with a dense, floral smell, steam mossing over the mirrors.

As the water ran, I remembered the bed we'd shared as boys, how Amit would be snoring while I confessed my attraction to Cleo from *The Catillac Cats*. I remembered riding on a plane to India when I was seven, and how Amit made me sit in the middle seat, next to a guy who kept ordering whiskey sours until he sauced all over me and my in-flight blanket. I remembered the nightmares after my mom died, how Amit would shake me gently by the shoulder, and sometimes, briefly, leave his hand there.

By the time I turned the faucet off, Amit was calling me, hoarsely.

I ran, almost tripped down the stairs. The television was off, but I found him staring at the blank, gray screen.

"I wet the bed," he said.

I stood there, waiting for something to happen.

"I wet the bed, Neel." His voice was low and stunned. "I thought I could hold it. I fell asleep, but I guess the beer . . ." He bent his head to his chest, his face crumpling. He began to cry without a sound.

"It's okay," I said. "Hold on."

I ran back to the upstairs bathroom and found a beach towel in the closet. When I returned with the towel, Amit was defeated, yielding. He let me peel away the blanket, his bathrobe, and his T-shirt, his damp scrubs and boxers. The smell stung. His knees were bonier than I remembered, a pale sheen to his calves. I threw a towel over him.

"Ready?" I slid my arms under him and gathered him up with a small groan. His skin was clammy, his legs impossibly heavy.

Pitching forward, I staggered up the stairs. In the hallway, we passed by Amit's old room, which gave off the neat, staid air of a museum exhibit. He swiveled his head around, hungrily absorbing all that he had missed for the past two months.

Finally, we reached the bathroom. Surprisingly, Amit didn't make fun of the bubble bath. He only said, "I know that smell."

Just when my arms seemed on the verge of giving out, I squatted, easing him into the water, towel and all. He held on to the sides of the tub, and I bunched two hand towels behind him so he wouldn't slip down. I caught sight of the surgical scar on his back, raised and pinkish, like a shiny, segmented worm.

"Is it too cold?" I asked, catching my breath.

"No." Amit lowered his head and closed his eyes. "It's nice."

He sighed. As his features loosened, I saw him forgetting his tears, our trek up here. "Thanks. You can go. Go do whatever you were doing."

I hovered over my brother. If I couldn't leave him then, I knew I never would.

I caught sight of my cloudy reflection in the mirror—a shadowy, motionless shape—and something landed heavily within me. Leaning against the tile, I listened to the gentle slosh of the water. I closed my eyes, and in an instant, we were at the pool again, Amit standing on the high dive, peering down, stiff with terror. The moment we locked eyes, his fear became my own.

Girl Marries Ghost

...

That year, thousands entered the lottery for only a handful of husbands. Of that handful, very few could remember what had happened after they had departed. One husband could recall only a smell: the stogie-scented leather of his father's Lincoln. Another had been stranded in an endless bed of his ex-wife's daffodils, and whenever he yanked a flower, two more plants unfurled in its place. Was it heaven through which they had passed, or some flavorless form of limbo? There was no one to ask, and gradually the question lost its novelty, eclipsed by the more pressing question of who among the living would land a ghost husband.

After Gina was notified over the phone that she had made it to Round Two, she filled out an online application whose seven personal essays and thirty short answers seemed a test of resolve more than anything else. She also taped the requisite Bio Video, doing the sorts of things that would set her apart from other grieving widows, like somersaulting on her backyard trampoline and baking a Kahlúa Bundt cake dusted with confectioners' sugar.

In a more serious segment, Gina placed the camera on the kitchen counter and laid out the basics of her life. Her husband had died in a bicycling accident last year. She was a stylist at Swift Clips, but without Jeremy's salary, she was having trouble meeting her mortgage payments. The bank guy had pitied her for a limited time and cut down her payments, but now, with the imminent rockslide of back taxes and late fees, her house, *their* house, would soon slip through her fingers.

Gina had to rewind and re-record the segment several times because she couldn't leak a single tear. Never when she needed it. At one point she got up, diced an onion, and when her eyes were properly bleary, she taped the winning take.

Three months later, the matchmaker came to Gina's house for what was termed the Final Round. Gina had expected a sage old woman with bad teeth and a soothing smile. The matchmaker's name was Barb Spindel. She wore her hair in a tight black bob and hugged her clipboard to her chest, as if to prevent anything from mussing her pin-striped blazer. She inspected a cracked photo frame, toed the rough shag carpet. She tilted her head at the coffee table, which was just a door resting on cinder blocks.

"Jeremy found it on the side of a street," Gina said with too much enthusiasm, tugging on the hem of her skirt. "Just laying on the grass. It was a real bitch, lugging it home."

Gina stopped. Barb was staring at her, eyebrows raised in anticipation of a point.

"I'm sorry," Gina said. "I'm nervous. I've read about ghost husbands, but I've never actually met one in person."

"That's what you think," Barb said. She lowered herself into a papasan chair, which creaked from her weight. With a blackberry fingernail, she tapped the bamboo frame.

"Can I ask a weird question?" Gina said.

"Please."

"Am I correct in assuming that none of these guys was ever a murderer? Because I don't think I'd connect very well with a murderer." From her pocket, Gina removed a folded piece of paper from which she read out other unsavories: suicides, addicts, wackjobs, felons. "Basically, I'm looking for someone without a whole lot of baggage."

"Gina, they all come with baggage. Lucky for you, this guy also comes with a very attractive dowry."

Barb told her about Hank Tolliver, born in 1935, expired in 1990. In life, Hank had been an orthopedic surgeon who died from a pulmonary embolism at age fifty-five. He had no children and one ex-wife: Helen.

Gina recognized his name from the Tolliver House, a country mansion of alabaster brick and gray shingle, with a tower that shot straight into the sky. As a little girl, when Gina's school bus passed the Tolliver House, she would press her nose against the window and imagine herself trapped in its fairy-tale tower, tall enough to skewer a cloud. "Hank has no heirs," Barb said in cajoling tones. "And he was smart enough to hire people to manage the house for ten years, in case he was to return. So if you two hit it off, the Tolliver House goes to you. If not . . ." Barb shrugged. "It goes to his second cousin Gardner, at the end of that ten-year period."

Gina stared at Hank's photo for a long time, trying to imagine herself beside such a beautiful man, in such a beautiful house. His hair was lush and combed back, his forehead broad, a faint raking of wrinkles at the corner of each eye. ("He looks sad," said Gina. "Oh, that's just his face," said Barb.) Gina sensed a kinship in his handsome, wounded gloom.

According to the terms of the contract, Hank would come home most evenings, like a normal husband, but the days would be hers alone. He would never expect her to have dinner waiting; ghosts did not eat. He would never want her to plump up with his child and set her life aside; ghosts did not engage in intercourse. Theirs would be an open marriage. "So you can tend to your carnal needs whenever necessary," Barb assured her. Gina gave a nervous laugh; Barb did not.

"Good. Great. Only . . ." Gina hesitated. "What if it doesn't work out?"

Barb paused to administer a disapproving look. "Financially, divorce is an unwise decision. Both parties lose everything." She explained how Gina would forfeit all the assets she had gained through the marriage, how Gina's ex would have to depart the world all over again. "Thus far, I've had an excellent track record, so I prefer to work with people who share my outlook on the bonds of marriage."

Gina nodded in solemn agreement.

Prior to their first date, Gina found on her doorstep a bowl of blushing peonies, with a note that said: *Looking forward! HT.* Somehow he had learned of her affection for peonies. As the days went by, her living room brimmed with a lush, leafy smell.

On a cloudless Saturday, she met Hank at the Tolliver House. When he opened the door, she stuttered her hello; he was so handsome. "Gina," he said, stepping aside to let her in, smiling as if he'd known her forever.

Hank toured her through every room. She opened the mottled burl doors of an antique Austrian armoire and leaned into the sweet stale smell. She cooled her palms against the marbled Jacuzzi across from a dressing table, where fruit-scented bath balls sat in a basket like a clutch of colored eggs.

"You don't have to show me everything," she said. "If it bores you."

"Bored?" He stroked the faded brass hinges on the bedroom door, each hinge engraved with a delicate fleur-de-lis. "I don't think I can get bored, not this time around. Everything feels new."

Gina found it hard not to stare at him. In a matter of minutes, he had capsized all her movie-fed notions of ghosts—the tattered clothes, the corroding flesh, the tortured soul. He looked polished, debonair, in loose slacks belted high around the waist, a polo shirt, and wingtip shoes that made no sound.

Finally he took her up the winding staircase of the alabaster tower. One great round window opened onto a park, where golf carts went whizzing across the green dips and swells, around the weeping willows, shivering their tresses. Hank had put on a Patsy Cline record, and Patsy's longing voice seemed to push faintly through the floor: *Oh, the wayward wind is a restless wind / A restless wind that yearns to wander . . .*

"Barb said you were married once," he said.

"I was. His name was Jeremy." She rushed through the rest. "He was riding his bicycle. There was a car. He wasn't wearing a helmet."

Grimacing, Hank removed a handkerchief from his pocket. For an alarming moment, Gina thought he was going to weep. Instead, he sneezed.

"Sorry," he said, after honking into his handkerchief. "About your husband."

She appreciated his insensitivity, how he didn't follow up with an oozy apology. Death was just another detail.

"Jeremy used handkerchiefs, too," she said, so quietly that Hank seemed not to have heard. He was looking down at the sidewalk, where a woman was tugging at her Labrador's leash. The dog was whimpering and wagging its tail. The woman flung a suspicious look up at Hank before scooping the dog into her arms and hurrying away.

Hank emptied a sigh at the glass. "People," he muttered.

"Do you know Jeremy? That was my husband's name. Jeremy."

Gina was about to add that Jeremy's eyes were blue at certain times and gray at others, but Hank said gently, "It doesn't work that way."

Gina nodded at her shoes, feeling stupid.

Gina's parents refused to travel up from Florida for the wedding. "You want to marry a ghost, then marry a ghost," her mother said over the phone. "Call me when you find your head."

"Mom, did you even read the article I sent you?"

Her mother gave an unconvincing grunt.

It was the same article that had first piqued Gina's interest in ghost marriage, and she'd even highlighted certain lines for her mother's edification: "In nineteenth-century China, it was perfectly acceptable for a young woman to marry a dead man, an arrangement called a 'ghost marriage,' which enabled families to consolidate their wealth and power and allowed enterprising young women to pursue their ambitions without the interference of a living husband or children." According to the article, the practice of ghost marriage was being revived in several parts of the United States. The statistics for the success of ghost marriages were quite high, and most women polled described themselves as "very satisfied" with their unions.

She sent the same article to her sister, Ami, who had manufactured an excuse so as not to attend the wedding. Apparently, she had volunteered long ago to chaperone her daughter's third-grade field trip to Shakertown, and she just couldn't leave the teachers hanging.

Gina supposed that Ami had a right to be annoyed. Ami's wedding had been carefully designed by their mother, and not one decision—from the choice of groom to the choice of boutonniere—had been settled without the opinions of Gina and her mother, followed by a nod from her father.

"Yeah, I read the article," said Ami, when Gina called. "But it's not like all these ghost marriages work out. What about that crazy woman with the diaries?"

"Mary," Gina said quietly. "Mary" was the sole counter-example, a woman who had fallen in love with her ghost husband "Mike." *If only I could get closer to him,* she had confided in her diary. She became obsessed with the idea of touching him, and it seemed to her that if humans could touch humans, then surely ghosts could touch ghosts. She shot herself in a Kroger parking lot.

"See?" Ami said. "They don't all have happy endings."

"But there's never a happy ending," Gina said.

Ami ignored the remark. "I don't know, Gina. I still think you could've held out a little longer. You never even tried Soulmates.com. Even I did Soulmates.com."

And on and on they went in circles of accusation and defense, like strands of hair swirling a drain, like sisters.

Hank and Gina married at the courthouse with Barb as their witness, as well as Lucille, Hank's former cleaning lady. Throughout the ceremony, Lucille stared at Hank in a dreamy daze, as if witness to a miracle. Afterward, they all stood outside the courthouse, glowing, and even Barb produced a close-lipped smile. "Thank you," Lucille whispered in Gina's ear, with a clenching hug. "Thank you for bringing him back to us. Call me when you need a cleaning."

Lucille then made the mistake of trying to hug Hank. No

one had told her that Hank couldn't be hugged; one could just as easily plant a kiss on a breeze. In her attempt, Lucille lost her balance and fell forward onto the sidewalk. Hank and Gina helped her to her feet, while a shaken Lucille brushed the gravel from her knees. "He can touch," Barb lectured, arms folded, "but he can't be touched."

After the wedding, Gina and Hank entered a period of sweet, cyclical domesticity. Sundays were Gina's favorite day, when she would bake muffins or biscuits while Hank sat at the breakfast table, reading the newspaper. Though he couldn't eat, he loved the smell of baked goods. ("The Bundt cake was my favorite part of your Bio Video," he told her.) Whether or not her cakes and muffins turned out, Hank was happy so long as the air was laced with butter and burnt sugar.

While the batter rose in the oven, Gina listened to Hank tell of the city as he had once known it. In high school, he lived around the corner from the Hilltop Theater, in the East End of town. The Hilltop was where he took his girlfriend on dates. He also liked hanging around Benny's Billiards, where he'd shoot pool or play cards or work the pinball machines until his mother called and had Benny send him home for dinner. There was no point in lying to Mrs. Tolliver about where he'd been; she knew by the traces of oil on his shoe soles, the same oil that Benny used to wax his floors.

Here, he laughed just like Jeremy—*Hah!*—a single huff that punctured her heart.

To Hank, Gina confessed her hope to someday open a sophisticated beauty parlor that would double as a bar. She had heard of such a place in New York, where a woman could sip from a martini in one hand and receive a manicure on the other. Why not in Louisville? She was sick of salons with names like Swift Clips and Mane Attraction. She envisioned a black-and-white tiled floor, counters edged in chrome. Hank loved the idea. He suggested a jukebox and maybe, on some nights, a live band. "I'll keep an eye out for spaces to rent," he said.

They talked all morning, until 11:00, at which point Hank gave her a brisk kiss on the cheek, put on his hat, and headed out the door.

After he left, Gina would garden, or watch TV, or try a cardio hip-hop DVD, hoping he wouldn't come home early and catch her in action. She had quit her job at Swift Clips, but she still made occasional house calls to her oldest clients, the ones for whom driving had become a hazard. Several of the women remembered Hank Tolliver. When Gina told Mrs. Fenton about Hank and his girlfriend going to the Hilltop Theater, Mrs. Fenton laughed. "Girlfriend or girlfriends?" she said. "I don't think he could keep track of them all, that old sly boots."

Whatever she did during the day, Gina always made sure to be home by 8:00 sharp. At that hour, a humid coolness would sweep through the house and a vapor would creep up the mirrors. She would hurry down the stairs, tracking the scent of smoked dirt as it grew more potent, until she found Hank hanging his trench coat in the closet. He always greeted her the same way: "Hey, kid, where ya been?"

But Hank seemed preoccupied in the evenings. Sometimes they played a board game or watched a movie, but most of the time he was in bed by nine. "All that walking," he'd say, though he never explained where he went, never asked her to join him. He simply wished her good night and retired to the guest room. In the contract, he had ceded the master bedroom to her, an arrangement she now regretted. She had never lain in a bed so big it made her lonely.

·

Over the next few days, Gina began to wake up earlier, thumping down the hall in the hopes that she would wake Hank. He seemed surprised to see her out of sweatpants, her hair up and fussy, pearl studs in her ears. Some nights she slept in rollers.

One morning, as Hank was folding up the newspaper, she asked if he might stay home tomorrow, since Ami was stopping by for lunch. Hank paused, smoothing his hand over the crease of the paper. "The sister who didn't come to the courthouse?"

"There was that field trip," Gina said quickly. "It might be nice for you both to get to know each other."

"She didn't want to know me before. Why now?"

"People change," she said. "I've changed."

"Yeah . . . ," he said, and looked away.

Gina stared at him, suddenly afraid of what he might say next. "Never mind. Forget it."

She got up from the table but was stayed by a subtle sensation across her palm. This was what it felt like when Hank took her hand, not the blunt force of human touch but something delicate, like a soft cloth wrapped around her skin.

"The contract said mornings and evenings, Gina. I can't be here whenever you want me to be."

She shook his hand off. "Where do you go all day?"

Abruptly, he rose from the table and said he had to get going. She felt a kiss glance off her cheek.

Watching him head for the door, she blurted, "I looked in the guest room last night. You weren't there."

Hank stopped. He turned halfway, his brow creased. "That's allowed. Check the contract."

He continued out the door, his peaty fragrance dissolving from the room.

Later that night, unable to sleep, Gina crept up the stairs to the guest room. The door was closed, a faint slip of light beneath it. She tapped her fingernail against the door. "Come in," he said.

Hank was sitting up in a bed so high, it required a wooden step stool to climb aboard. He wore red plaid pajamas. The bedside lamp brightened the side of his face and the cover of the book he was reading: *The Count of Monte Cristo.*

Hank lowered his glasses. "Hello, warden."

He watched her walk to the other side of the bed and climb on top of the covers.

"Gina—"

"I tried Ambien, I tried counting sheep. Nothing works." She peeled back the comforter and wiggled her way in until she was laying on her back, the sheets pulled up to her chin. She closed her eyes. When Hank began to protest, she whispered, "Just five minutes."

She kept her eyes closed. After a moment's pause, she heard the book thump shut and the click of the lamplight. She felt him settle noiselessly into bed. He didn't move.

"Why did you and Helen divorce?" she asked.

Hank gave a long, bored sigh. "I fooled around on her. More than once."

"Do you know what happened to her?"

"Nope."

"And you don't want to know?"

Hank rubbed his eyes. "Come on, Gina. We shouldn't talk about that stuff. You read the Primer."

Gina had skimmed it. *A Primer to Interlife Relationships.* She had found its tone condescendingly bright. *Too much looking back will lead to a nasty case of whiplash. Leave past relationships in the past.*

In a small voice, Gina asked if he ever missed Helen.

Hank flung off the covers and hopped out of bed. "It might be the mattress that's keeping you up," he said. "Sleep here tonight. See if you like this one better."

Tucking his book under his arm, he left.

The next day, Ami came over for brunch. Gina toured her around the garden and pointed out the tomatoes that had just begun to plump. She liked them green and taut, lightly fuzzed in down, like newborns. Ami kept wrapping her sweater tighter and asking, "Is he here? Can he see us?"

Gina pinched a tomato from the vine and moved on, pretending not to hear. Ami and her family lived in a grand colonial house with a hot tub whose novelty had worn off among the kids, leaving her to dutifully boil alone once a week. Gina suspected that Ami was jealous, now that hers was no longer the larger house.

"All right, fine, I'm sorry," Ami said. "It's not that I'm against you marrying a ghost, in theory. I just don't know anybody who's done that. It's a generational thing. Maybe in fifty years our kids will look back and think we were just a bunch of uptight assholes."

"If we make it that far."

"Just tell me you have a plan. If something goes wrong."

It wasn't the first time Ami had raised that concern. Normally Gina would have dismissed her sister, assured her that everything would be fine. But the night before had left Gina with questions that took root in the fertile dark, and by morning had flourished into the inevitable: Hank was having an affair with Helen. Two weeks ago, this would have meant much less to Gina. But lately she'd found herself dwelling on him when he wasn't around, thinking ahead to what they might discuss the next day. She was frustrated by his reticence in the evenings, when he returned to her slightly sad, and yet somehow fortified.

"I could divorce him," Gina said. An image came to her, of Hank tracing his finger over the fleur-de-lis hinge. "But no, I couldn't do that to him."

"Why?" Ami's eyes widened with more wonder than worry. "What would happen to Hank?"

"He'd go back there. Wherever he came from." Gina wrenched a handful of sinewy weeds from the earth, wrung the dirt from their roots. "And I'd lose everything—the money, the house, the cars."

"You could move in with me. Till you get your sea legs."

"My legs are fine right here, Ami. This is my home."

Ami bit her lip without reply. She drew a hand through Gina's hair and twisted a lock around her finger like a vine. "Is that why you did this, Gina? For the house?"

"And someone to play Scrabble with."

Ami released a curl, rested her hand on Gina's shoulder. "No one could beat Jeremy at Scrabble."

"No one but me."

After Ami left, Gina went snooping around the house. Not snooping, she told herself, just a form of spousal tourism, harmless to the delicate ecosystem of their marriage.

But Hank wasn't making it easy. He had eradicated the house of nearly every portrait and photo frame, an absence she had never noticed before. The Primer had talked a lot about making new memories, but completely razing the old seemed extreme.

She turned to her laptop and Googled "Helen Tolliver."

There was only one Helen Tolliver (now Helen Tolliver Dade) who was originally from Louisville, Kentucky. She was featured in *The Springfield Gazette* for earning blue ribbons at the Third Annual Pie Festival, where her mocha pecan won the Nut category and Amateur Best in Show. Her new husband, George, remarked: "I'd eat that pie off the floor, it's so good." But the article showed only pictures of pies, not people.

Gina climbed the spiral staircase up to the tower, where Hank had brought her on their first date. Back then she had noticed the cardboard boxes and crates stacked up against one wall, but only now did she choose to open them one by one. She rooted through the trophies, diplomas, Boy Scout badges, a plastic rhinoceros, a framed certificate from the Rotary Club of Louisville, and a 1963 *Playboy* sheathed in plastic featuring "The Nudest Jayne Mansfield." At last she came across a leather photo album with *Our Wedding* embossed in gold on the cover. She opened it.

Helen. Helen was beautiful. She wore a boat-neck dress with elbow-length gloves and lofty hair that lengthened her neck. In nearly every picture Hank was glancing her way and laughing, as if he had just discovered a woman whose sense of humor outdid his own. The reception looked like a Derby party—bourbon in Mason jars and mint juleps in silver cups; lavish sun hats, pale pink neckties, careless charm.

As she flipped the pages, Gina felt shame and envy sinking in her stomach like stones, as if her snooping had taken her too far, as if Helen were looking right back at her, transmitting some silent message through her innocent smile. *You weren't invited,* Helen said. *You want memories? Find your own.*

What came to Gina was a day like any other, when she and Jeremy were in the park, lying on their backs over soft spring grass. He was reading a magazine while Gina watched the blue-brown currents of the Ohio River and its sprawling clots of driftwood, dislodged by yesterday's rain, gliding downstream like the backs of ancient sea creatures.

She was beginning to doze off when Jeremy made a noise. "Hm," he said, as if he were having a conversation with the magazine. With her ear on his shoulder, Gina felt his voice ripple through her, like a seismic wave. *"Mm."*

She raised her head. "I can't sleep when you do that."

"Do what?"

"When you go, *Mm, Mmmm.*"

He laughed. "I didn't even notice I was doing it. Okay, I'll be quiet."

She nestled herself against his chest, and he went back to reading. But now the silence felt strange. Gina raised her head again. "What are you reading?"

"Your diary," Jeremy said, without removing his eyes from the magazine. "'Dear Diary, I am the luckiest woman in the world to be married to a guy who puts up with my shushing. He's a patient man. And he looks like a male model.'"

She smiled. "A male model?"

"'I heart him so much.'"

"I have never 'hearted' anything."

"'I just wish I could lay around with him forever.'"

The grass stirred. They went back to being quiet. Gina put her ear to the cavern of Jeremy's chest, felt the twitching of his heart beneath his secondhand soccer jersey. All those organs carrying on their precious work until one day, like that, they wouldn't.

Out of the blue, Jeremy kissed her hair and said, "Oh, all right, I heart you, too."

·

In the late afternoon, Gina sat in the gazebo and watched shadows lean across the grass. She swirled the melted shards of ice in her vodka tonic. Drinking alone, in the daytime, wasn't part of her usual routine, but in an hour or so, she would confront Hank, and a glass of watered-down courage might help.

What would she say to him? That she loved him, against all the odds? Play that Patsy Cline record in the background, that tune about railroad tracks and broken hearts? Some sentiments were better left in song. She poured herself another drink.

For hours, Gina waited, glancing at the mirrors for the first breath of vapor. Hank never came. She baked a tray of fudge brownies from the box, filling the air with warmth and chocolate, while her stomach remained uneasy.

Around eight, the phone rang. She snatched it up.

It was a man whose voice was higher than Hank's, but heavy with authority. "Yeah, hi, is this Gina Tolliver?"

"Yes," she said, her voice suddenly clogged with fear. "Yes, I'm her."

"Are you related to Hank Tolliver?"

"He's my husband. What is it?"

"Can you come get him, please?" He stressed the word *please,* as if it were the last scrap of courtesy he had left. "He's in my son's tree house, and he won't come out. He scared the crap outta my kid, I don't know how long he's been in there. He even pulled up the rope ladder."

"Why?"

"Heck if I know. He keeps asking if he can stay up there for a while. He's not hurting anybody, but he won't come down. He said his name was Hank Tolliver, and I looked him up in the white pages. The only Tolliver is you."

"I'm his wife," Gina said, and then repeated herself, this time, more firmly. "I'm his wife. I'm coming."

•

The tree house was quaint, wedged between the branches of a knobby oak. Gina stood beneath it and called up to Hank. "I just want to talk," she said.

A dejected voice emerged from within. "Is Cro Magnon Man with you?"

"His name is Mr. Adler." She couldn't remember his first name though Cro Magnon seemed apt, in light of his sloping forehead and the ledgelike brow over his eyes. "This is his house."

"It used to be Helen's house."

"Either way, we're trespassing. The only reason Mr. Adler hasn't called the cops yet is because his wife feels sorry for us."

"I feel sorry for her, too."

"Can you at least drop the ladder? It's just me."

After a few moments of silence, a rope ladder wobbled down.

Gina removed her flip-flops and clambered up the rungs. She hoisted herself belly first into the tree house, only to find Hank hunched in the corner, sitting cross-legged, his elbows on his knees. He was wearing navy socks. Exposed, they made him look like a giant, graceless boy.

Gina sat in the opposite corner and waited for Hank to speak. She noticed a stack of newspapers beside him, all comics and crosswords beneath his gray felt fedora.

"This *was* Helen's house," Hank said finally, as if they'd been arguing through the silence. "Five fifteen Burnham Heights. She moved in after we separated." He peered through the cut-out window. Mr. Adler stood at the back door, his arms crossed in a territorial fashion.

Hank sighed, then spoke in a softer voice. "She said she didn't want anything to do with me or my money. She wanted to start over completely. So she bought this place, got a job at the library. I used to take the long way home sometimes, just to drive past her house. To see her without her seeing me."

Gina tore a dry leaf to pieces. "So this is where you've been every day? Peeping from some kid's tree house?"

Hank lowered his gaze. Maybe it was the dimming light, but his eyes had never looked more swollen. "Here or the library."

"Did you find her there?"

"Oh no. She probably retired a long time ago."

"Well, she also remarried, if you want to know the truth."

Hank bowed his head. Gina almost wished she could take back the news, but she continued, quickly, hoping to minimize the pain. "I looked her up on the Web."

"What web?"

"I think she lives in Illinois, but who knows, she could've moved again. She could have grandkids. She could be dead. You have no idea!"

Hank blinked, quietly processing the news. He returned his gaze to the window, calm as the day Gina first met him. "Sometimes I think I see her in the kitchen, like before. I know it's probably not her, but it's a possibility. It's better than nothing at all." Hank looked at Gina. "I think you know the feeling."

Gina leaned back against the wall, averting her gaze so he wouldn't see her tearing up. She concentrated on the potpourri of dried leaf in her palm. Yes, that was a feeling she knew very well.

While Hank waited in the passenger seat of the car, Gina apologized to Mr. Adler, promising that Hank wouldn't frequent the tree house anymore. As she drove Hank home, he stared straight ahead with the unseeing eyes of a statue, the brim of his fedora pulled down.

Gina gripped the wheel with both hands as she tunneled through the fog. The car bobbed up and down hills, swung around sickled trees, not a single taillight or streetlamp to guide the way. Here she was, crawling along with Hank beside her, and never more frightened, more alone.

At last Gina pulled into the half-circle driveway, but she didn't turn off the car. They sat without speaking. She looked out the window at her pale, glowing house.

She remembered moving into Jeremy's house and how it shocked her, all the noises he made. Horking into the sink, or retorting at talk radio, or belting out the chorus of a song. It drove her crazy. Once, she heard a violently loud slapping sound coming from the bathroom. She knocked. He stood there, bare-chested, baffled, lotion on his hands. "What?" he said. "I'm just lotioning." That was the story she had wanted to tell at his funeral, but she didn't know if anyone would find comfort in it, or how to explain why she did.

And now dread filled her chest at the thought of this silent house looming before her, and all the silent afternoons to come.

Gina told Hank of her promise to Mr. Adler, that he wouldn't return to the tree house anymore.

"I can't promise that," Hank said finally.

Gina nodded. For a moment, they said nothing.

Hank placed his hand on the door handle. "Coming?"

"You go ahead," she said.

"Scrabble?"

"Not tonight. I need some rest."

"Tomorrow, then."

Gina shook her head.

Hank lightly knocked his knuckles against the door. "I think I'll put on a record."

Their eyes met, and Gina's stomach clenched. "I'm sorry, Hank."

He gave a small shrug, and then: "We tried."

She watched him enter the house.

After he closed the door, Gina continued around the driveway and idled at the curb. She looked up at the tower's round, lit window like a second yellow moon. For an instant, she felt herself again on the front step of the Tolliver House, giddy and hopeful, about to meet Hank for the very first time. It wasn't simply the house that had wooed her, or the cars, or the money, or even his cinematic smile. In marrying Hank, she thought she could marry herself to a realm where Jeremy still existed, even if only as the faintest echo between her ears.

Gina turned onto the street, in the direction of her sister's house. She took a narrow, empty road. Halfway there, she was stopped at a red light when she began to weep. *Move on!* Ami whispered in one ear. *Wait, come back,* Jeremy said in the other. And though no one was around, Gina pressed both hands to her car horn for three whole seconds. She then sat, breath held, in the silence.

Acknowledgments

...

My heartfelt thanks to Nicole Aragi and Jordan Pavlin for their friendship and guidance. Thank you also to Christie Hauser, Leslie Levine, and the wonderful Knopf team. My friends and teachers from Columbia University put their effort and wisdom into these stories, with excellent last-minute assists by Jenny Assef, Alena Graedon, Nellie Hermann, and Karen Thompson. I am grateful to the Maru family for their open arms. Hannah Tinti, Maribeth Batcha, and Dave Daley—thank you.

I am indebted to John Macarthy, lead paralegal of Timap for Justice and section chief of Bo Town, who provided much useful expertise for "What to Do with Henry," as did Frans de Waal's *Chimpanzee Politics*.

Gama the Great and his brother Imam are historical persons, and in imagining a slice of their lives, I drew from the following sources: *The Wrestler's Body* by Joseph S. Alter; *Strong Men over the Years* by S. Muzumdar; and "The Lion of the Punjab" by Graham Noble, from *InYo: Journal of Alternative Perspectives on the Martial Arts and Sciences* (May 2002).

The magazine quote in "Girl Marries Ghost" is from "Hitched" by Ariel Levy, a book review that appeared in the January 11, 2010, issue of *The New Yorker.*

And finally, my love and gratitude to my parents, for endless gifts; to Neena, Raj, and Christy, close readers and closest friends; and to Vivek, for entertaining this hermit with fruit, good humor, and good care.

A Note About the Author

• • •

Tania James is the author of the novel *Atlas of Unknowns*. She has received fellowships from the Fulbright Foundation and the DC Commission on the Arts and Humanities. She was raised in Louisville, Kentucky, and now lives in Washington, D.C.

A Note on the Type

· · ·

The text of this book was set in Sabon, a typeface designed in 1966 by Jan Tschichold (1902–1974), the well-known German typographer. Based on the original designs by Claude Garamond (ca. 1480–1561), Sabon was named for the punch cutter Jacques Sabon, who brought Garamond's matrices to Frankfurt.

Typeset by Scribe
Allentown, Pennsylvania

Printed and bound by RR Donnelley
Harrisonburg, Virginia

Designed by Laura Crossin